Edited by Lynsey Hawkins

YoungWriters
First published in Great Britain in 2007 by:
Young Writers
Remus House
Coltsfoot Drive
Peterborough
PE2 9JX
Telephone: 01733 890066
Website: www.youngwriters.co.uk

SB ISBN 1-84602-705-5

Foreword

Young Writers was established in 1991 to promote poetry and nurture the creative writing talent in school children across the UK and overseas. Today we continue to provide a platform for children and young adults to showcase their work. Our ghost story competition has proved so popular over the last few years it has become an open competition. Now we receive hundreds of stories all year round and publish 4 or 5 ghost story books a year!

Terrifying Tales is a collection of ghost stories that will certainly give you the creeps! From friendly ghosts and Hallowe'en adventures to the gruesome and macabre, the young writers in this anthology showcase their story-telling talents. The best ghost story wins a family ticket to either London, York or Edinburgh Dungeons, with 2 runners-up each winning a Staedtler Writing Set and a selection of books. Congratulations to our winners, and thank you to all our authors for being part of this fantastic anthology.

Contents

The Creative Writing

Well done Kate!

Congratulations Kate, your creepy short story wins you a fantastic family ticket to London, York or Edinburgh Dungeons! These fantastic places have become incredibly popular tourist attractions despite the fact that they are filled with grisely exhibitions and examples of atrocities from British and European history. The museums appeal to our morbid curiosity, but be warned - they are not recommended to those with a nervous disposition or squeamish nature!

The museums have been brought right up to date with the latest in multi media displays and modern equipment to aid visual and audio displays. Take a walk along a Victorian street which allows you to uncover gruesome reality of the infamous Jack the Ripper's crimes. If you feel that you can cope with more, see how the barbaric punishments of the british past were executed including boiling, drowning and torture under the reigns of Henry III and those during the French Revolution. A new attraction is a recreation of the effects of the Great Plague which struck Britain in the seventeenth century. Whichever Dungeon experience you choose to visit Kate, you are sure to have a terrific and terrifying time!

The Painting

For the past year, she'd been living alone. Her new home was isolated. No other houses were in a mile radius, and there were no main roads for forty minutes. Even then, the roads were narrow and a large vehicle would have trouble getting down them. When she'd moved in, she'd had phones installed and lighting installed. She didn't want to be writing or painting by candlelight. On Mondays she went to pick up her shopping and her post.

One week, when she got home after her trip to the village, she absently opened her post. She had a parcel from London and thought it might be from her brother. When she opened it, she took out a small canvas painting, almost exactly the same as the one she had just finished painting and was sitting on the easel in front of her. There were differences. The sky was blood-red instead of warm orange. The woman was crying instead of smiling, she was holding a clean dagger instead of a poppy. There was also a poem enclosed. It was an adaptation of her recent poem. All the light had been sucked out of it. The words had been swapped to bring a dark, shadowed meaning to it. The doorbell rang and she was still reading the poem.

Nobody had told her about the spirits that took the souls in the house. They only came every five years.

Two weeks later, they found her, the picture on the easel was that of the crying woman, with blood dripping from her dagger.

Kate Bertram (15)
Bryanston School, Blandford

Hooves Of Blood

Riding schools: joyful, loveable and filled with laughing children. It's quite a different story when it has been abandoned. The sight of death stares you in the face with every footstep you take towards it. No door, smashed windows and gunshot holes in the crumbling roof. One shaking step towards this ghostly riding school is one step to your fate. In the woods that run alongside you, a shadow slides from one tree to another.

No one is around you, though you can still hear the sounds of children laughing and a horse trotting. The sound deepens in tone, the horse scuffs its hooves and the child screams. Silence. Until the roaring sound of gunshots cut through the roof, like a knife through your heart. Your eyes are drawn to the left to see - standing in mud - a girl and a horse covered in blood and still dripping. They run, run towards you faster than any living creature could run. Closer and closer. So close you can hear them breathe. Shivers and chills run down your spine. I can't even decribe the nightmare-like images that spin round your head. Closing your eyes will not help - only to open and catch sight of them lying in a puddle of blood.

Once in everyone's life they will ask themselves this very simple question: 'What does it feel like to die?' This place doesn't tell you, it shows you.

Holly Johns (12)

Well done Holly!

Your scary story wins you a selection of books and a 15-piece STAEDTLER gel pen set.

Well done Emily!

Your scary story wins you a selection of books and a 15-piece STAEDTLER gel pen set.

Bloodthirsty

Holly turned off the computer, picking up her handbag. Swiftly she click-clacked her way towards reception in her high heels. She stopped by the desk, scowling. There was nobody there.

A door creaked. Holly turned - and the crumpled form of the guard flew past, smashing against the wall where he sank to the floor, leaving a crimson stain. Holly scrambled behind the desk as a second figure appeared. Her blood ran cold as be bent down and lifted the guard. He used only one hand. He gave a faint smile. Holly saw the glimmer of very white teeth, and shuddered. His eyes were vivid green, ringed with navy. His red hair was spiked up with gel.

The man turned slightly, with the guard dangling from his fist. Holly swallowed as he leaned forward to whisper something in the guard's ear - who, though only semi-concious, let out a howl.

As Holly watched, a forked tongue slipped between the man's lips and tasted the beads of sweat upon the guard's neck. The man opened his mouth, thin lips sliding back over pointed teeth. Gently he touched his fangs to the security guard's throat. And then, his eyes narrowing - he bit down.

The security guard let out a shriek that died with a gurgling sound as blood bubbled in his throat. Holly flung herself flat, listening to the thump as the dead man's body hit the floor. Insane laughter echoed - and then the lights went out.

Amy Townsend (14)

Woman In The Cemetery

There she was yet again, for the fourth time this week. Creeping through the forest, aware of nothing around her. She must have been searching for something or someone in Spooksville Cemetery or else she'd be mad. Who would want to come to this life-scarring disaster for a walk in the moonlight? Nobody. That's for sure.

However, through the cemetery she sauntered carrying gloom with her. Sadness enveloped her tired, crooked, bent-double body and tears filled her sunken-in eyes. Her hair looked like it had been combed with a fork, and it hid most of her pale, wrinkled face. She expressed a look of confusion and was puzzled. The rags she wore were dirty and torn and hung off her thin, frail, fragile body.

Slowly, she staggered past each gravestone, becoming more secretive, mysterious and suspicious with every step that she took. She paused occasionally and glanced behind her at the forest in the distance. The trees there were bare and they bent towards each other in the fading moonlight as though hiding something from the world. Perhaps she was expecting to see someone?

It was hard to tell what she was thinking exactly but it was certain that she needed help. Help from the disastrous mess that she called 'life'. Help to assist her in discovering what she needed to find. Help from the devastating memories that brought tears to her eyes. But that help would have to arrive another night for as soon as the moon disappeared, she went with it. She evaporated into thin air.

Heather Kernot (13)

The Finger Of Death

The clock struck twelve. Bethany lay in her bed, too frightened to move. She glanced over at her bedside table to see the time. It was 12.01. Was this is? Had the terror that had haunted her every night finally disappeared? There was only one answer to the question and even she knew the answer was no. The door creaked open, a bony hand appeared, a screaming sound started to wail and the face covered in blood began to speak.

'On the 31st night of the tenth month the curse will be lifted and you will never need to be scared of me again,' wailed the ghost.

Bethany breathed a sigh of relief. Confused by the ghost's words, she tried to fall asleep. Would she soon be safe from this horror? Only time would tell.

It was the 31st October and Bethany couldn't wait to get to bed. After all these years she would be free of the ghost. The clock showed 11.59. The old grandfather clock downstairs began to chime. But once again the door creaked, the bony hand appeared and a screaming noise began to wail. Everything that happened next was just a blur to Bethany. All she could see was red.

The next morning Bethany's mum came to wake her daughter up. As she entered the room, she knew something was wrong. Instead of her daughter, all that could be seen was a pool of blood and what looked like a long bony finger.

Rachel Joanne Carney (13)

A Ghost's Life

Imagine a place where new people come every second, but no one goes, no one changes. It would be scary, but that is my life.

Every day I wonder what he is like and what she is like, my brother and sister. You see I died when I was eleven, a car hit me, now I'm a ghost. I've wondered how my family are, so this is my quest to find them.

Someone told me if you close your eyes, think of a person and turn around once you will see them. I tried it and there he was, my brother, in another world about twenty years old with a child. 'Well I know he is happy, I'll see if my sister is happy.'

Ring, ring. 'Hello,' my sister picked up the phone, someone at the other end said what they had to and put the phone down. My sister started to cry. 'What's wrong?' I said, it made her jump. When she saw me, she pinched herself, and went quiet.

Then she said, 'What! You can't be here, you're dead.' She stopped, took a breath and said, 'That was Mum, Dad's died.' That made me sad and I cried, all of a sudden I was back in my world. There was Dad, I went to him and hugged him, I didn't want to leave my dad so I never tried to get back.

Soon Mum came, then my sister and then my brother.

Rita Griffiths (12)

Rising Of The Dead

One evening Mark Adams slept until the sound of breaking gravestones woke him. Mark went to the graveyard; the gate chains were broken, Mark slowly entered. He asked, 'Is anyone there?' There was no answer. He saw human-shaped shadows wherever he looked. Mark was terrified, but obsessed with carrying on.

A gravestone moved, nervously he peered over it; suddenly a bony hand grabbed his leg, slowly piercing it. Mark was screaming trying to pull his leg away. Mark escaped, limping away, shouting, 'Help!'

Mark could not stand on his wounded leg anymore, he was in complete agony. Luckily Mark was right outside his house. He crawled to the door, opened it and got inside, as he closed it, half-decayed bodies entered his driveway. Mark slammed the door, struggled upstairs and found his shotgun. He sat on the top step staring at figures banging on his door.

After 2 hours the banging stopped. Mark climbed downstairs, he opened the letterbox, and he could see nobody. He opened the door, one of the undead came from nowhere. Mark blew off his head, but more came. One grabbed Mark's gun, another came forward and bit chunks of his flesh. Blood dripped from the mouths of their decayed faces, some walked with broken ankles. Mark passed out in agony.

Police searched for Mark, all that could be found was a patch of dried blood and one of Mark's shoes. Strange happenings sometimes occurred again, but nobody ever knew what was going on.

Henry Thompson (14)

The Hut

I was exhausted, sweat was pouring down my face. I was completely lost. Where could I go now?

In the distance I noticed a hut that I was sure hadn't been there before, but as it was the only shelter from the hammering rain, it would be better than nothing.

As I entered the dingy hut I left the door open, for it was the only light I could get, as there were no windows. Strangely, even though it was raining hard, the moon shone bright in the sky.

The hut looked very bare and lonely. Its one room had a hole in one corner, probably the toilet and a broken pipe in the wall where the sink should have been.

In another corner there was a straw mattress. As I looked to my right, I saw the sink broken on the floor, it had been thrown two or three metres across the floor. In the middle of the room there was a dinner table laid out, but it had been left in a hurry because a glass had been knocked over and there was a toppled over chair beside it.

The floorboards creaked as I moved across them and I became afraid that they would break under me at any moment.

Suddenly the moonlight had disappeared and as I turned to face the door, I saw a large man, his face was covered by shadows. As he turned and closed the door, there was darkness ...

Alison Fellgett (13)

The Velvet Cloak

Darkness wrapped its velvet cloak upon the dead. An owl rustled in a nearby tree, its yellow eyes searching the emptiness.

A gentle patter of delicate feet sounded down the overgrown lane. A figure approached, dressed in a dark hooded cloak and carrying a couple of withering flowers. Their colours were masked under the heaviness of the night, as though the last drop of life had been drained from their delicate forms.

The figure walked quickly, light-footed upon the dusty gravel of the graveyard.

The owl still rustled in the tree, still seeking its unlucky prey. Moonlight caught the face of the figure; pale and delicate in the curtained night. The young woman approached an old stone grave, placing her small, bony hand upon its ageing frame. She bowed her head for a moment, her breathing quick rasps that produced a misty smoke, evaporating into icy air.

Silently now, the woman knelt and placed the withered flowers at the base of the grave. She muttered a few words that were lost upon a growing breeze. Gathering herself together, the woman glided swiftly from the graveyard, the moonlight occasionally capturing her secretive beauty.

Darkness continued to close in, as she disappeared into the night.

Emily Harris (16)

Dreams

I was walking home on a cold, misty winter's night, when I felt a cold hand rest on my shoulder. I turned. No one was there. I carried on, thinking it was my imagination. The snow started to fall, making me long for my warm comfy bed. I felt like there was someone strange watching me. 'Stop scaring yourself,' I scolded. 'There's nothing there and you know it.'

If only I had been right.

Later in the week, I was tossing and turning and trying to sleep. Suddenly a cold chill ran down my spine and I sat straight upright. That's when I knew. Whatever it was, it wanted *me*. It had to be. The only thing I didn't know was *why?*

Things had been OK for a while. No nightmares. No more scares. Phew. What a relief! I was relaxing more and letting my guard down. It was Thursday and I was on my way to my night shift. Silently, a dark shadow stepped out in front of me. I pushed it away and ran. It caught hold of me and I struggled. I could hear my mum shouting my name, 'Tasha. Tasha!' I couldn't see her though. Suddenly she was there and then I realised. It was all just a crazy dream.

Rebecca Wilson (12)

Haunted

The stairs creaked as Monica came down. *Bang! Bang! Bang! went the door. 1.25am, who could that be at this time of night?* She opened the door. Nothing. Monica was wide-awake by this time so she went into the living room to read a book. As soon as she sat down, *bang! Bang! Bang!* She raced to the door. Nothing. *Right,* she thought, *I'll get a dining chair and sit outside to catch the pranksters.*

She grabbed a chair and the phone, she placed her chair on the front decking and dialled her brother's mobile, telling him to come asap. She sat down. Monica heard footsteps walking up and down the decking. She turned to her left. Nothing. She turned to her right ... 'Argh!'

The clock struck 4.27am as Robert turned up. He pulled up in his Land Rover and raced to the house. The front door was open. Strange. He walked up the steps to find his sister draped over her chair arm, her nightdress soaked in blood. A cold wind blew around him. A warm breath on his neck. He spun around ... 'Argh!' He slumped at the feet of Monica.

Jemma Clarkson (12)

Play

The door creaked open.

'Hello, is anyone there?' No one answered. I climbed out of bed and opened the door. There was a creak on the attic stairs. I slowly walked up to the attic door. I pushed the door open and a draught of stale air hit my face. I could hear someone crying so I called out, 'Is anybody there?' There was no answer but I heard the crying stop. I entered the room and looked around. 'Hello?'

I saw a figure moving towards me. It looked like a child wearing a white nightgown but it was floating across the floor. I felt my pulse increase, this was not natural. The child opened its mouth and I cringed back but all that happened was that I heard a voice say: 'Have you come to play?'

'Yes I have.' I didn't know where that came from, it wasn't me. My feet started to move towards the child. I couldn't help it.

'Good.'

I stopped right in front of the child who looked like a young girl. She opened her mouth and there were holes in her teeth and gums that were infested with maggots and spiders. Her tongue was a lump of decaying flesh that occasionally flicked from side to side.

I couldn't tear my eyes away. As she opened her mouth wider and wider, it became a black pit of despair sucking my soul away.

She walked to breakfast in my body. She had stolen my life.

Amy Livingstone (12)

Fear

Have you ever been afraid? No. Well you should be! Why? I hear you ask. Let me tell you ...

It all starts in a normal bedroom, in a normal house. The owner of this bedroom is a fifteen-year-old teenager. Her name is Sophia. She isn't afraid, but she should be. Her house sits on top of a spiritual nexus. Every one thousand years this nexus opens up to let out the spirits of past and present, and these spirits are not happy.

This very day on which we are living, this nexus is ready to open again. They will hunt for fresh victims and fresh souls to take with them back into the nexus. As the tear widens, the sun goes down and light becomes but a fragment of a dream. Screams tear through the house shattering windows and blowing out the eardrums of the four members of Sophia's family.

There is a blinding whiteness enveloping the family and they huddle together in the blistering coldness of the light. As the light settles and the wind speeds up, they see clouds, or spirits drifting towards them. Sophia's father is the first to be caught by one of these vile, evil beings. Her mother can only scream as the three of them see her father torn limb from limb and blood is painted across the walls, then he is gone.

Then her mother screams as she is ravaged by mutant beings of a distant parallel universe, then she is gone. Then the coldness is gone and the lights are gone and the howls and screams are gone and Sophia clings to her brother as they find themselves alone in the bloody mess of their parents.

Now are you afraid? How do you know your house isn't above the same nexus ready to tear your life apart, literally?

Kerry Menning (15)

Ghost Lake

The lake had received its name for a reason and I am about to tell you how it got its name. It started on a dark and dreary winter's evening ...

It was a horrible day, the weather, it could *not* look any more *miserable* if it had tried. There was a low mist across the lake and there was not a soul in sight. That was when I saw it. It came to me with great speed, it was horrible, it had great big eyes and an unforgiving smile. I ran, through the trees, through the town centre, no one seemed to have a care in the world that a great big *thing* was chasing after me.

I finally arrived at my house, the heavens opened! It was raining cats and dogs, my mother came to the door, she asked me why I was looking so dazed. I turned around there was nothing there, just a grey-black puddle, on the floor ...

What had happened? Was it even there in the first place?

Luke Williams (13)

The Dare

I gently opened the gate, my long brown hair blowing in the dusty night-time wind. I stumbled down the stone path, clumsily tripping over uneven rocks scattered along the way. The wind was howling hard and leaves were rustling past my feet. I got to the door and looked up. Mounted on the wall, surrounded by overgrown ivy, was a chipped plaque that read: *Number 13.* Shivers raced down my spine.

I carefully opened the battered door and entered the house. It smelt damp and rotten. I glanced around. Pictures hung crookedly on the walls; thickly layered with dust. There were cobwebs in every corner of the ceiling and damp was running down the walls.

I slowly walked along the hallway, the floorboards creaking every step I took. My heart started to beat faster and faster. I felt sick.

Suddenly there was a loud *thud!* and the door slammed shut. I jumped. My heart was pounding so fast, I felt as though I was going to burst.

As I turned to look behind, I thought to myself, *why did I do this stupid dare?*

Ellen Thomas (13)

The Inner Asylum

Cold burning at the back of my head. My brain swelling, ready to burst and paint the wall red. The spine-ripping nightmares in your bed. It is red fire burning out of your mouth.

When you feel the pain, it brings a hollowing, screaming roar, burning to get out because it's being strangled. You may not look like you're in pain but it hides inside waiting ... waiting to pour out all over streets and down the gutter. It comes down the pipes and back into your veins. Heating you, melting you. It is insanity getting the better of you. It is insanity getting the better of you. It is your oxygen turning into liquid around you. Drowning in a pool of horror.

And, as your burning tears come down, they pull your face off with them. Your screaming shows you are weak, you will be tortured more - all that - but remember, it's all in your chaotic mind ...

Sean Cloherty-Rogers (10)

Tap, Tap, Tap

I lay in bed, listening to the tapping on my window. I didn't dare sit up and look, but peered over the edge of my comforter, eyes wide.

Was the window open? A shimmering white passed over my field of vision and I suppressed a scream. I didn't believe in ghosts.

The door creaked open a centimetre.

Did it?

The sound stopped, my eyes darted. A cold breath touched me. I went icy.

Another creak from the door. I breathed harder as a white shape played on the wall. Shadows moved at night, not lights.

But ghosts did.

Sweat broke on my forehead. I raised my head. *Tap, tap, tap.* 'Who's tapping at my window?' I whispered.

No response. Just a tap, tap, tap. Could ghosts tap like normal people? Dunno. Not going to find out.

I got to the door before I remembered how it had moved in a breeze that wasn't there.

'Mom?' I croaked. Couldn't go past the door. Couldn't go back to bed - though goodness knows I wanted to. Couldn't turn around to see what was at my window.

There were no trees planted along my side of the house. *Tap, tap, tap.* My room was on the second floor. *Tap, tap, tap*.

If I didn't look, it might get me. But I was too scared of what I might see.

I didn't turn around. And I never found out who was knocking at my window.

Tap, tap, tap.

Kathryn Dueck

The Woods

I always thought the wood a welcoming place where you had a picnic with your teddies. I could not believe how wrong I was. I only found that out on the day I died.

I guess I should have listened to my mum. She had told me never to go into the woods alone and I never knew why she said that. Of course being 14 and all, meant that I didn't listen to a thing my parents said, so one day coming home from school, I jumped over the wall and into the woods.

I walked for 10 minutes and everything was fine until I came to an open area. I stopped to see where to go next when suddenly a figure appeared of a small girl who seemed to be in Victorian-style clothing. Then a madman with an axe came up behind her and chopped her head off, but they just seemed to fade away. It was silent until a voice broke it by shouting, 'Timber!' It sounded like it came from behind me so I turned to see the mad axe man standing behind a falling tree. The tree came straight for me and flattened me. It wasn't until a man walking his dog was in the woods before somebody found me, squashed into the ground.

If you go down in the woods today, you'll get a big surprise, if you go down in the woods today, you might even die.

Georgia Moore (12)

Deceased!

I spun around at the sound of the door exploding open behind me.

Five men in black leather jackets and balaclavas came through shouting for everyone to get on the floor. I froze in horror as I realised what was happening.

Suddenly I noticed that there was nothing between me and the door. I saw that I wasn't being watched so I carefully and quietly tiptoed towards the door, in a few steps I was there.

Then I saw the guard and his gun, I gasped and he turned and saw me.

There was a loud bang as he pulled the trigger. I was thrown backwards and there was pain in my chest.

My breathing was abnormal; I couldn't take a proper breath. I was beginning to feel dizzy and sick. There was a funny taste in my mouth and pins and needles in my limbs. There was a lot of talking and everything sounded very loud. My vision had become very blurry. Suddenly I felt incredibly cold and tired.

Everything was turning black; I looked around trying to see something, anything. Ahead I could see a small, bright speck of light. The speck of light was growing bigger as each second passed. The pain in my chest was slowly disappearing. Then I blacked out.

When I awoke the pain had receded. I was in a strange room; I looked around and stopped with shock as I saw myself on a table naked and realised I was dead.

Chloe Chapman (12)

The Ghost Ship

Two men were out fishing one night when a fierce storm arose. The two men were sure to be killed when a large ship appeared. The men were not at all scared but relieved when they saw it.

They climbed aboard the ship and saw there was a hole in the deck and the mast was torn. They walked over and saw the captain leaning over the wheel. They went over to him and slowly turned his body around, it was a skeleton.

The wheel kept on moving and steering the ship, the torn mast was being put up and the deck was being cleaned but nobody was doing these things. The two men were terrified and ran backwards and forwards on the deck. Everywhere they looked jobs were being done, but there was no one to be seen.

They went down to the lower deck and they found more skeletons lying on the ground. Many with bullets and knife blades in them. Then they heard people talking and laughing in one of the cabins. They were so relieved they found someone, but when they opened the cabin door, the noise continued but nobody was there. The men were so scared, they ran to the top deck and looked for their ship but it was smashed to pieces.

The men were driven to insanity and killed themselves. Their ghosts joined the other ghosts on the ship and sailed round the oceans forever looking for more victims to join them.

Daniel Carrington (12)

The Night Killer

'There's post for you!' shouted Kim. Kim was Ellie's little sister. Ellie rushed to the door and stuffed the letter in her bag. At school, she met up with her friend, Donna. Suddenly, she remembered her letter.

'I got a letter this morning. It was a bit weird because I don't normally get letters,' she said.

'Oh well, just open the envelope,' Donna moaned. The letter inside read: *'Beware: These are your last three days!'* Ellie was speechless. They didn't talk for the whole day. Ellie went straight to sleep after her homework.

For the next two days, the letters came again. On the third day a letter came saying: *'This is your last day!'* Ellie was trembling. She didn't take part in anything at school. After school, Ellie invited Donna to her house. They played until nine and then did their homework. When it was late, Donna decided to go home. She only lived a few doors away. Afterwards, Ellie went to sleep. Then Donna went back to Ellie's house to get the book that she had forgotten. The front door was open, so she just went upstairs. Ellie's room light was off so she just walked in, got her book and went.

The next day, there were policemen all around Ellie's house. Donna was astounded. On her bedroom mirror, there were these words written in blood:

'It's good you didn't turn on the light yesterday'.

Ellie's murder was a mystery.

Simran Dhanjal (9)

The Woman In The Classroom

I just sat there, scared for my life. I was the only one who could see it. Standing in the middle of the room, was the ghost of a Victorian woman, glaring into the back of everyone's heads. She looked as if she had been drowned, her steel-grey hair coming out of her tight bun. Suddenly her pearly eyes fixed on me, she knew that I could see her. She started drifting over towards me, her arm outstretched; her gnarled fingers were just about to grab me when the teacher hit me. 'Stop daydreaming and get on with your work!' she yelled.

I did as I was told, but when she wasn't looking, I glanced over my shoulder. No ghost, no old woman.

Hours later I was walking home from school. All was fine, until it went dark; I was by the River Thames when it started. Everything went quiet, silence, apart from the water lapping against the bank. I started backing away from the street, towards the river. Suddenly gnarled, old hands grabbed my shoulders and pulled me into the freezing water. I struggled against their vice-like grip but they were just dragging me down, away from the light. I turned around; there was the woman, the woman from the classroom. I was paralysed, staring into those cruel, heartless eyes. The darkness was closing in around me. I could feel my heart pounding. *Thump, thump, thump, thump, thump, thump ... silence.*

Laura Allen (12)

The House

The voice hissed through the dark wood, seeping through branches of twisted trees. There was no escape. It froze the listeners to the spot and crept icily over their skin. Looking up into the dark Manor of Blood.

'My voice will cry out through these walls and my blood will cry murder! This house will be cursed forever and so will be thy spiteful town.'

That night they went. No one came back out of those warped iron gates those brave souls went in, in vain and all inspiration of the truth faded. Even little Timmy went in.

Three years later a shadow came over the town. The town became dark. Little children were taken in the dead of night and those not killed were haunted by mere death itself holding on to any shred of hope left until they were called to the Manor of Blood by immorality.

'My voice will cry out through the walls and my blood will cry murder! This house will be cursed forever and so will be thy spiteful town.'

I guess no one will ever know what was in that house as the town fell down below.

That was a legend in my old town until the night that the moon never came out and the owls were silent, a boy came whispering. *'His voice will cry out through the walls and his blood will cry murder. This house will be cursed forever and so will be thy spiteful town.'*

Timmy was his name.

Sophie Jardine (13)

The Ghost Gardener

The factory where Max worked was put on short time, so Max decided to get another job.

After looking through the paper he saw a vacancy for a gardener at the Manor house. He was not deterred by the fact he didn't know much about gardening and went for the interview. He got the job because he was the only applicant. He was told he could plant and grow how he liked as long as everything was tidy and presentable, first he had to clear the ground of weeds and dig so he could plant. Max was gaining all of his information from books at the library.

One day as he was working at the Manor house there was a man leaning against the wall. He started telling Max good places to plant the vegetables and Max was pleased to have the advice because the old man seemed to know what he was talking about. In time he introduced himself and told Max his name was George. From that day on, the old man came every day and Max looked forward to his visits.

The next day, Mrs Digby, the owner of the Manor house, came out to congratulate Max on how good the garden looked after six months of working. She told him she was a little puzzled after looking at old photographs of the garden. 'It's amazing, you have laid out the garden just like our old gardener did before he died. His name was George.'

Hollie Bailey (12)

I Don't Believe It

'David!' called Frank. 'Come back, it's haunted!'

'I don't believe it,' said Frank, making his way in. Rumours of a ghost haunting the woods didn't stop David; he was determined to prove to Frank, *there was no such things as ghosts.*

The trees made eerie rustling noises and twigs cracked beneath his trainers, he looked around, it looked spooky enough.

All of a sudden, something grabbed his shoulder. He screamed and turned around. He pushed it away and began rushing frantically for an exit. He ran into any direction with it, which happened to be a 500-year-old spirit of a girl following after him.

As he went further in, the spirit followed and appeared in front of him. He walked backwards and stumbled over a large stone. It towered over him and took his soul.

500 years later

'Have you heard of that ghost haunting the woods?' said Elena. 'He entered hundreds of years ago, and hasn't returned.'

'Yeah right!' said Katie.

'Katie, come back,' said Elena, 'it's haunted!'

'I don't believe it ...'

Maryam Bhayat (12)

The Deserted House

The air that night had a slight chill, which made my spine shudder as I walked down the empty street. There was a rustling of the trees, the wind began to howl, it was the night of Hallowe'en. This was it, the house, number thirteen, they always said number thirteen was an unlucky number.

I stood there for a while as the wind ran through my hair, I could feel a slight unwantedness drift round me as I walked through a thick blanket of mist.

I opened the ancient rusted gate half hanging off its hinges, the grass was so long, I felt like I was walking through a maze of snakes trying each time to grab every time the wind blew.

This was it, the door, I could only see it a little, as ivy covered it like a mother of a baby trying to stop trespassers like me trying to open it.

But there it was, painted in front of me, the number thirteen in white paint: I was scared, in fact, terrified, my legs felt like jelly as I reached for the door ...

Holly Dormer (12)

The Beast

This is a story of death and devastation. A story of a boy and a girl. This is a story of the beast.

Tom was woken by a strange howling. He looked outside, he saw a full moon gleaming in the jet-black sky. He looked down and saw the silver light spill on a black, hairy, red-eyed, what looked like a -

'Tom breakfast!'

School was boring as usual, maths, English, science, Tom and his friend Anna were walking home until Tom saw a big, black, hairy, red-eyed wolf. He turned around and then looked back, the wolf had gone. 'Tom look!' screamed Anna as they approached the street, Tom turned his head and saw a house up in smoke and fire. He immediately recognised the house, it was his.

Tom's face turned white.

'What happened?' asked Anna,

'It's my parents ... they're dead.'

After the funeral, things went crazy, his next-door neighbour went missing, he was found at the bottom of a river with a knife in his back. A tree fell down and killed a cat, another day a little boy fell in a lake and drowned. But the strange thing was the wolf he had seen was at the scene of every death.

One day he went out with his uncle. They got out of the car and then a massive wolf pounced on his uncle, and slaughtered him in front of Tom.

'You're going to die!' said an evil voice.

Tom disintegrated, the beast though was gone, it melted as Tom died.

Jack Maidment (11)

Was It A Dream?

I sat up scared, out of breath, was it a dream, yes, no, yes, no? I didn't know. I ran to my mum's bedroom shivering, I was freezing. There was no one in my mum's room. I tiptoed to my sister Amy's room, she wasn't there. Maybe she was in my big brother Sam's room. Maybe they're in there, all together, a big happy family, who was I kidding?

No, no sign of anyone, my brother, sister or Mum. Then I remembered Charles, my baby brother, he was only one, a little baby with a big life ahead of him. I carefully lifted him out of his cot, he was freezing, I couldn't hear him breathing.

I ran downstairs hugging Charles tight to my chest, as I ran into the front room, I saw my mum, laying there not breathing, I was so scared, I ran around the sofa to the phone, there were my brother and sister. I picked up the phone, rang 999, then put blankets and duvets over my dying family. As I heard the loud siren, I heard a crash, *bang!* 'Argh help!' I saw my family as ghosts yet they were lying on the floor in front of me.

Amber Maurice (10)

My Grandfather's Diary

The sky was like a demon from Hell shadowing the world as I set out on my quest to find my grandfather's diary. The cold wind sent shivers down my spine, as I finally found the courage to knock on the colossal doors of the towering castle. I crept into a hallway of darkness and mystery. I wanted to leave immediately, but I knew I had to look first. Suddenly there was a movement upstairs. 'Is anyone there?' I whispered as my heart started beating so hard that I was sure that it would burst out of my chest. There was no answer so I climbed the winding stairs to reach an empty room.

There was a desk covered in cobwebs and dust. I walked slowly towards it but I slipped and fell down a trapdoor, which was hidden under a Chinese rug. I found myself in a small room, it was some type of basement or cellar. As I looked around, I saw a ladder, it led to another room above, so I climbed up to reach the first floor.

I heard a scream from upstairs and ran straight out the door not taking a single look back. I was so frightened that I hardly remember how I got home.

The next day when I looked in my rucksack for my schoolbooks, I found my grandfather's diary, hidden away at the bottom. Where did that come from?

Tierney Martin (11)

Bad Moonlight

'Fine! If we're gonna argue about my face and how ugly it looks, we may as well just not be friends at all! I hate you Amy!'

'No Ali, she didn't mean it like that and you know it!' my best mate Kelly shouted, but it was too late.

I had taken what was meant to be a joke, dead seriously again, except in my eyes, a joke doesn't include how big my nose is. We had just been to seek Amy and she was wearing an extremely short nightie and found it funny, then her exact words were, 'At least I don't have a pointy nose.'

I ran to the park and sat in the tree where the three of us had sat on the day we had met, a few years ago. I never realised how creepy the tree was, for it was dripping with bats and damp moss was coating its rough bark.

The full moon caught my eye. It suddenly seemed very cold as the wind danced down my naked arms. I raised my small hands up to my supposedly abnormal-sized nose. A tear ran down my freckled face.

'A teardrop hurts the moonlight!' a whisper echoed around me.

Was I imagining things?

'The moonlight must get its revenge!'

Obviously I wasn't.

I jumped down in a rush, as a frosty, ghost-like figure shot through my body. I hit the cold, wet ground with a thud. I was going ...

Going ...

Gone.

Samantha Softley (12)

Return Fare

Becky sat waiting with her friends anticipating what was to come. They sat shivering with excitement in Becky's bedroom, the ouija board sitting in front of them with their fingers pressed tightly to the glass.

'Is anyone there?' Becky asked in a shaky voice.

Apart from the low whistle of the wind outside, nothing changed. The girls shared looks of embarrassment for scaring themselves - then collapsed with laughter and let go of the glass.

'Guys!' one of them cried through tears, 'Let go and anything that came through is stuck with us!'

'Don't be silly,' Natalie sighed calming down. 'Nothing came through - we were scared for nothing.'

They grinned sheepishly and played more games, before settling down for bed.

Becky awoke less than an hour later. The dark seemed tangible as though something was there but she shook the feeling off and walked downstairs to the kitchen. Her feet hit the freezing stone of the kitchen floor and a shudder ran up her body, a figure looming ahead of her in the narrow space shone a perfect white. Its eyes seemed black, hollow and burning.

'Let me back ...' Its voice sounded like a vague echo as it started forward. Cold air rushed as it passed through her body - its cold form dragging though her mind seeing inside her very soul - and it was gone. She was found in the morning frozen on the stone floor. The price for returning to the spirit world - to take another with you.

Natasha Wraight (15)

Ghost Trouble

Once upon a time there were two children, Ellie and Harry. One day Harry said to Ellie, 'We should go on an adventure!'

'Yeah!' shouted Ellie, so they went to the back garden (so their mother wouldn't know they were going on an adventure) and saw a fence and they thought, *that's the only way out without Mum knowing.* Ellie saw a gap and said, 'There's a gap,' so they ran through it and saw ... a big giant forest. They ran through and at the very back of the forest they saw a haunted house and saw a ghost.

'Argh!' they shouted at exactly the same time, they ran around the haunted house, sprinted into the attic and saw five more ghosts.

'What is going on here?' screamed Harry, so they hid under the old, mouldy bed but a ghost came after them and grabbed them. It took them to his hideout and tied them to a large pole and the ghost left them alone.

Ellie found a knife in her pocket and cut the rope in half and they ran home. She saw her mum was a ghost. 'Mum, is that you?' shouted Harry.

'Whoooo!' screeched the ghost.

'Let's go to Grandad's house,' they both shouted together. So they sprinted to their grandad's house, but Grandad was a ghost.

'Everyone is a ghost today, what will happen if they are ghosts tomorrow?' worried Ellie.

'I don't know,' answered Harry.

They sprinted to their auntie's house and saw she was a ghost as well so they ran home, grabbed Mum and took her to the ghost's hideout. There they saw this strange man and Ellie was shaking, 'Who are you?'

'I turn ghosts back to humans!' said the man.

'Just what we need,' said Ellie. 'Can you do it for us?'

'Of course I will,' said the man so he sat each of Harry's and Ellie's family in special chairs that zapped them back to normal again. In 5 minutes, everyone was normal again.

'Thank you so much!'

So they all went and had dinner at Harry's and Ellie's house.

Jessica Ford (8)

Egyptian Hallowe'en

October 29th - 8pm - Spooky Pyramids

I hate my brother! I mean, Michael keeps saying I'm scared. In the uncharted pyramids? I, Virginia Clarke, am not scared of some brainless dead people. The only reason Michael thinks I'm scared is because I want out of here by 12am tomorrow (I have my reasons).

The explorer with us, Robert Fox, says we should get some sleep, he's an Egyptian you know, but I will say no more!

October 30th - 8.30am - Same place

I would rather have slept on than eat breakfast because it was revolting. Robert says its meat covered in herbs and spices. It tastes like mud! Robert and Michael want to dig and discover the unknown, so I'm tagging along.

3 minutes later

We've just entered a small chamber. It has a very damp musty smell about it. There are stains on the walls and ancient Egyptian writing. I can only speak 4 words of Ancient Egyptian - *Death come unto you.*

The smell is so sickening. I keep thinking someone recently died in here, well, that smell must have been here for over 3,000 years! That's because this place is a tomb. Seriously.

October 30th - 7pm

I'm officially spooked now. A wind just blew through our shelter, but it sounded like Ancient Egyptian: *'Death come unto you!'*

I told Michael and Robert so we're trying to find a way out. *We're lost, we're lost, we're lost, we're ...*

A loud groaning and shuffling echoes around us.

Mummies ...

Kayleigh Park (13)

Mrs Higgins' Sweet Shop

Mrs Higgins' sweet shop is the all-time favourite of the children in St Claire's, although most agree that they're not quite right. Mrs Higgins' sweet shop sells beetle humbugs and bloodthirsty lollies, it sells screeching gobstoppers and rotten toffee apples, you could buy squirming liquorice or frogs' ears pips, there's jaw-locking chewing gum and toe-growing chocolate or you could experiment with the three-legged mints (the name's self-explanatory).

No one quite knows how Mrs Higgins became quite so famous, but the children are odd and the adults are worse. So anyone with half a brain cell knows not to go to St Claire's (even to window shop) for you may never leave. So nobody goes to the little village anymore. It is strange though Mr Higgins made ordinary candy which Mrs Higgins sold, but now they're both gone but sweets are still sold through a gap in the wall and Mr and Mrs Higgins are never to be seen. So who sells the sweets at Mrs Higgins' sweet shop?

Rhiannon Bowen (13)

Sarah's Wardrobe

Giggling, Sarah closed her wardrobe doors; she hoped the seeker wouldn't find her here. The light was drained from her surroundings but she wasn't scared - yet.

She couldn't hear any of her family so she thought none of them had been found. Feeling alone Sarah decided to look in all her jacket pockets for something to fiddle with but before she could even lift her hand, she heard a cold little girlish whisper. 'Get out,' it said.

Sarah ignored it, thinking she'd imagined it, but she heard it again, this time she felt its breath on the back of her neck.

'Get out, now!'

'What? Who are you?' asked Sarah with a shaking voice. She was really scared now, her heart pounding. She turned around and could see a white outline of a head. Sarah tried to open her wardrobe doors but they were stuck. She pushed harder, not taking her eyes off the figure moving closer and closer towards her.

'Get out!' it screamed.

'I'm trying!' roared Sarah even louder. She banged and banged at the doors but they didn't move, the strange creature was moving closer. Sarah began to feel faint, hot and clammy.

The next day police found the whole of Sarah's family brutally murdered. Sarah included. Were they killed by the ghostly figure in Sarah's wardrobe or was it trying to protect her by meaning get out of the house, not of the wardrobe?

Nicola Morrison (14)

Through The Transparent Face

Rain lashed against the windows. Loud crackling thunder sounded. Lightning flashed across the sky. The lights flickered off. The smell of burning wood wafted through the house.

A young terrified girl felt her way to the corner of the room. Smoke slowly filled the room. Her dry mouth hung wide. It wasn't smoke, it was ghosts. Beads of sweat dripped down her fair face. Green eyes pierced the dark.

As quick as it had all started, it was over. The lights came on and the ghosts disappeared. They might have gone but one image stayed in the girl's mind. She had seen that face before, but where? She decided to go to bed. At least there nothing could attack. The boy though, he was so familiar. Where had he come from?

Tossing and turning. Crying and screaming. The ghost rose the girl from her nightmare. Shaking like jelly she sat up, she sat up straight. He was there again. She wasn't scared anymore, she felt excited. He wasn't out to hurt her but to help and protect. Although it was too early, the birds weren't even singing, she rushed quietly to the bookcase.

Pulling dusty family photo albums off the shelves, she sat flicking through them, just when she had given up all hope of finding a name to the transparent face, she found him. Sat right at the front of a wedding photo, Jaime Stockford smiled back. That was her name, her name.

Flicking forwards through the photo album, as though fast-forwarding time, Jaime grew and grew and then nothing, emptiness. In his last black and white photo he was a 14 years old, with green eyes and a pale face.

Chelsea Johnson (14)

Hiding From The Beast

My story starts like any other, on a dark scary night. I was running as fast as I could and hadn't stopped for what seemed like forever. I knew I would have to stop soon to catch my breath. There was a cold, icy breeze in the air but sweat still ran down my face. The dark sky made the atmosphere much more frightening. I could see the graveyard up ahead. I started to speed up. The stitch in my side digging into me. My heart thumped so hard that I thought it might explode.

I finally hid behind a big enough gravestone. I was breathing so hard that I was desperate to catch my breath before the beast heard me. I sat there listening to how quiet it suddenly was. It was then that I noticed how cold it was getting. I could feel something strange on my neck, as if someone was breathing down on me. I slowly looked up and to my horror, saw the beast glaring down at me with a greedy grin. It's mouth wide open, drooling and showing its sharp yellow teeth. I started running again, not knowing what else to do. I ran all the way to my front door. I ran inside, locked the door and ran up to my room. Finally I was safe.

I turned round to face my room, and guess what? The beast was staring right at me. I thought, *this is definitely not my lucky day!*

Kimberley Hamon (13)

Playroom

'Come on you wimp, open it.'

'OK. OK. The handle is stiffs,' said Zehi.

'Oh let me try,' Jelena said.

'Way cool!' stated Zehi, moving around the attic.

'We could come here to play after school,' Jelena said, placing the china dolls on the rocking chair.

'Hey, you guys, your mother has been calling you for your dinner,' a large man said, standing in the doorway.

'Oh Daddy, could we have this as our den?' Jelena asked running to her daddy.

'I don't see why not,' their father said, shutting the door.

Zehi opened the door of the attic and walked in. 'Not again!' All the toys were over the floor. 'It happens every time!'

'We must have a ghost,' Jelena said, laughing.

'I'm not a ghost, I live here,' a voice called. 'And I'm quite annoyed with someone. This is my playroom.'

'Who are you?' stammered Zehi.

'I am Amelia Johnson and I live here! Who are you?'

'I am Jelena and this is my brother Zehi.'

'Oh. What are these? I have never seen toys like these,' said Amelia pointing to a computer. 'It looks fun.'

'That's what we use to amuse ourselves,' said Jelena.

'What did you do in the evening?' asked Zehi.

'Mama would play the piano and someone would sing or someone would read. Sometimes we were taught needlework. I liked it best when Thomas read to us, he brought the books alive.'

Elizabeth Rose Cowell (14)

Full Moon

I take a further step on the moors. I am ready. I am cloaked in black, and hooded. I stop. I am here. I watch the moon rise. The full moon. I whisper one word. 'Moonlight …'

I begin to transform. My legs broaden. I feel my head elongating. I slip off my coat. I am not cold, as I am growing fur. I am transforming. My ears lengthen into a point. My clothes split, and fall to the ground. I need them no more, I relish this feeling. I only get to do this one night a month. I grow claws, and then at last my fangs come. It is done. I am in my true form. I utter a long, heartfelt howl. I am the greatest being on the Earth. I turn around and bound to the nearest village. I never tire. My stamina never runs out … until morning.

I am at the village in seconds. Everybody is sleeping, except one man, and a wolf. The man has just killed and robbed a woman. He is in an alleyway, counting his loot. He looks nervous, edgy … and tasty, so does the body.

Suddenly, the killing instinct takes over, I howl, and move in for the kill. He barely has time to scream. A short yell, then I howl and pounce. I bite his neck, breaking it. I shake the body, showering me with blood. He is dead. I feed …

Charlie Alcock (11)

Drowned

Always the same questions. 'How?' It's always how. 'How can you deal with them? How can you work there?' By 'them' they mean the bodies and by 'there' they mean the morgue, of course they do. I'll tell you. I don't 'deal with them', I just never show it.

I hate it when we get a kid. It kills me. This one, Charlotte Wood, drowned. In her pool. They say her mum did it. She's been arrested. I disagree, but I don't judge. I just cut up the stiffs.

I was sat by her, filling in the report, when I looked at her. Charlotte Wood. Poor kid.

'Hello.'

I jumped. (I work in the morgue, what do you expect?)

'Kids shouldn't be ...' I stopped. For one thing, she was transparent. For another, she looked an awful lot like ... 'Charlotte,' I choked, in need I say, utter shock.

'How do you know my name?' Before waiting for an answer, she said. 'Where's Mummy?'

'They think she pushed you in the pool. Is that what happened?'

She started to cry. 'She didn't do it! She didn't! She didn't! Mummy didn't do it! She never would! She went to the dry cleaners, the lady there will tell you! She told me to stay away from the pool, I'm sorry! I'm sorry! Please don't spank me. I'm sorry!' she sobbed. 'I want my mummy!'

'You'll see your mummy real soon ...' I choked, very nearly crying.

She sniffled and vanished.

Aidan C Milan (12)

An Unwelcome Visitor ...

I see her in the filled basin, in the mirror, out of the window. Her cold eyes. Occasionally I doubt if she's real because as soon as I turn around, she is gone.

'Brush your teeth, Ellie!' called Mum.

'Have you taken the bathroom mirrors down?' I asked cautiously ...

After cuddling me in bed, Mum switched off the light.

Everything was silent, until the singing started. I tried to sleep, but it was hard to ignore, 'La-la-la-la-la,' in a mocking voice.

Then I saw her, not a reflection but the real thing. My nightmare in reality. This time I knew what she planned to do. Her dry white hand, that was usually stretched out to grasp, was holding a rusty dagger.

I tried screaming, but no sound came out. I thought about running, but I was trapped in bed with her gliding closer, still singing eerily ... Then, it was all over.

No, my guardian angel had not rescued me, it was finished. She drew the dagger up over her head, looking at me through her grey, snakish eyes. She plunged the dagger deep into my throat, a satisfied smile on her face.

That was it, my life ended at 10. No future. No hope.

I awoke the next morning shaking, thinking it was a dream. I went downstairs to say good morning to Mum, and to ask for my birthday presents. But when she saw me, she screamed.

I looked in the mirror, no longer afraid.

Emily Morley (11)

Rat Attack

It was a pitch-black, foggy winter's night with the ghostly white moon as the only light. On this particular night, deep into the heart of the thick, murky wood something bone-chillingly terrible was happening.

Rob and Jimmy entered the wood with caution, beneath their feet, twigs kept snapping, it made Jimmy jump out of his skin. It was getting darker by the minute and very spooky, alarm bells were ringing inside Jimmy's head but regardless he ignored them. By now, every tree looked like petrifying monsters about to grab them and tear them up limb from limb. Jimmy was constantly looking over his shoulder whereas Rob was made of stronger stuff and carried on walking with no worries whatsoever. Strange noises echoed through the wood making Jimmy's heart stop. 'What was that?' Jimmy squeaked shaking Rob's arm.

'Oh it's just the wind! Stop being such a coward,' sighed Rob.

Jimmy carried on walking, though taking smaller steps this time.

Something king-sized, black and furry scuttled over Jimmy's leather shoe. He let out a high-pitched scream which made Rob turn around with a face like thunder, 'Shut up! You're giving me a heartache, now stop being such a wimp,' Rob cried. Jimmy lowered his head in shame. They ventured further into the wood, Rob had longer legs than Jimmy and was striding ahead into the fuzzy distance.

'Wait up Rob!' Jimmy shouted in despair, but his weak voice was lost in the wind.

Jimmy was completely alone, or so he thought. He fell to his knees not daring to move. It was pitch-black now because the moon had disappeared behind a layer of thick fog. He was surrounded by glowing red, non-blinking eyes. Just there, watching him.

Jimmy felt his bony knees knocking, he was numb with fear. He tried to shout but no sound came out. The owners of the stone-cold, beady eyes shattered the silence to pieces with a mighty shriek and jumped on to Jimmy digging their razor-sharp claws into his back, ripping the flesh and tearing it apart.

Through the blinding pain Jimmy realised that the vile, black, hairy monsters that surrounded him were giant rats. They had teeth like swords, a custard-yellow colour filled with deadly disease. Their fat black bodies were smothered in buzzing flies and there were sticks sticking out of their ruffled, scraggly fur. Jimmy tried to run, but it was impossible as there were two evil giant rats holding him down.

Suddenly there was a stab of pain and Jimmy lay motionless in a sea of deep red blood, the rats started to devour Jimmy. His guts flew everywhere and blood splattered on the surrounding trees.

Louise Elliott (12)

The Bleeding Heart

Recently, a family moved into a beautiful mansion. They had one daughter named Elizabeth. Before going to bed, Elizabeth went to the kitchen to get a glass of milk when she saw a girl with blonde hair and skin as white as snow walking, with a bleeding heart in her hand and a hole in her chest. Elizabeth was terrified and she started to scream and run, but the ghost didn't go away, she just kept walking with her bleeding heard gripped in her hand.

Elizabeth ran to her parents' room hoping that the girl would disappear, but she didn't, she kept following her, and even her parents started screaming. They asked her why she was following them, but the only thing she said was 'heart'. Even though the family was terrified, they tried to sleep.

The next morning Elizabeth and her parents went to the local library to find information about the mansion and about the family who'd lived there. They found out that there was a girl called Elizabeth who was murdered there and that they'd never figured out who'd killed her. They also found out that she'd been found with her heart cut out of her chest and that the family bribed the police so that they wouldn't investigate the case. The family decided to ask the ghost who'd killed her and tell the police.

When the family got back to the mansion, they waited until it was dark to try to find out who'd killed the girl. When the girl finally appeared, they asked her who had murdered her and she said, 'Mother and father.' After she said that, she walked away and disappeared. The family ran to their car and drove as fast as they could to the police station. When they got there, Elizabeth told the police everything that had happened and the police closed the case.

Arturo Sigüenza-Samuels (11)

The Forgotten Child

It was one cold and frosty winter's night when a girl named Sarah was babysitting like usual for her mum.

Sarah's parents went out on a romantic date for their anniversary so Sarah was left all alone with a baby in a huge, dark and spooky house, waiting for the homecoming of her mum and dad.

Tip-tip-tip, there was a noise from upstairs. 'Whiskers is that you?' whispered Sarah, who thought the noise was her cat. 'Whiskers!' she whispered again. All of a sudden Sarah heard voices from above moving closer and closer downstairs. She ran towards the kitchen and hid in the kitchen cabinets.

'Sarah ... Sarah ...' a voice gasped spookily and turned the kitchen light on.

'Go away, please go away!' Sarah had been saying in her mind but instead blurted it out.

The noise had vanished and Sarah had appeared out of the cabinet, slowly tiptoeing out of the kitchen and up the stairs, going to see if the baby was alright.

She finally got up the stairs, 'Oh thank God, you're OK!'

Sarah picked up the baby, but she really picked up a demon child who'd taken over her baby sister's body.

Two hours later, Sarah's parents arrived home but had a feeling that there was something very different in the way their baby looked at them when they arrived home.

Normally she'd start laughing but today instead of laughing, the baby gave an evil smirk and sneered as they passed.

When Sarah's parents went to kiss her goodnight, the baby was gone and all that was left was blood dripping off the ceiling and writing on the walls.

Sarah's room was empty as well, all that was there was a body which was hung up against the outside of the window and a baby sitting in her bed eyeing the girl with a roar of laughter.

Then the doors shut behind the parents, they were doomed, what happened to them, no one knows, all that was left was the guts of two humans around the bedroom and a stream of blood flowing down the stairs into the wine cellar.

Sheriece Nagar (12)

Honey, I'm Home!

The creaking of an opening door filled the house. 'Honey, I'm home,' shouted Mrs Petunia, from the front door. She had come back from her weekly visit to the spa. There was no answer. Mrs Petunia dropped her bags inside the doorway and looked in every room in the house, for her husband Sedrick. She heard a screech from outside. She ran to the back door and saw nothing unusual, just the same old flowers, trees ... and the garden shed!

Mrs Petunia walked slowly towards the garden shed. She opened the door, to find her dear Sedrick on the floor in a puddle of blood, with both his wrists and neck slit wide open. She got down on her knees to cuddle Sedrick, and burst out crying. She then looked up, focused her cloudy eyes on the wall of the shed, and saw something very irregular...

There was writing on the wall, not just any writing, it was threatening and wrote in blood. It read: *'I will be back, so be on your guard!'*

Mrs Petunia broke out into even more tears.

That night, (after the police and everyone had been) Mrs Petunia was all alone in the house, with no one but her dog Fido. She was sitting on the sofa, when she heard a faint voice, she didn't hear what the voice said, but sat there petrified. She held a cushion to her chest and whispered, 'Speak up you wimp!' The voice was louder and clearer this time, it said, 'Get out of my house, before something terrible happens!

Fido started whimpering and crawled under the table. Mrs Petunia said, 'Where will I go? I mean, erm ... I live here!' There was no answer but a light breeze swept the room, causing the door to slam shut. Mrs Petunia went to open it again but it was stuck.

A faint outline of a man was standing right behind her, with an axe! Mrs Petunia screamed and ran to the door, she started banging on the door, pulling at the door handle and yelling at the top of her voice. *Help!* No one heard her, she turned around and there was the man with the axe, Mrs Petunia's head dropped to the floor with a thump. There was an evil cackle, then ... silence!

Anyone seen going into the house never came out again! *Ha, ha, ha!*

Laura Grady (12)

A Long Night

In 1993, a girl named Gina always went on a girls' camp in the summer holidays. She went with her four friends, Courtney, Molly, Kimberlie and Lisa. This year when she went it seemed very much the same, but it wasn't Gina had been hearing noises coming from the shed that hadn't been opened in years. She was just brushing her teeth before she went to bed and as she was walking to the dormitory, she heard someone or something whispering her name. 'Gina! Gina!' It repeated and all of a sudden someone touched her shoulder, she turned around, no one was there.

She told herself over and over again, *it's just my imagination.* Gina then went back to the dormitory.

'Oh I've forgotten my toothbrush!' She went back, entered the toilets and noticed she was the only person there and the door closed just as if someone had walked in. Gina looked around, she didn't see anything but a moving shadow. She walked up steadily and slowly. 'Argh!' She screamed, her best friend Courtney was hanging off the showerhead, her fingers, arms and legs chopped off, her throat had been cut with a sharp knife. Gina stood there watching her best friend die, crying herself to death.

Courtney tried saying something but Gina couldn't make it out. Gina tried helping her but it was too late, she had gone.

Gina turned around to go and get some help but a slim, ugly, weird- looking man in a Hallowe'en costume blocked her way and started slashing her. When he was finished, he got them both into a black bag and dragged them away. He took them far, far away where nobody would know where they were and that is the end of the story. Gina and Courtney were never to be seen again.

Hayley Pedge (12)

Run!

My life was a strange life, every now and then something went missing. Every now and then there was a creak in the floorboard, a rustle in the attic. I asked Mum and Dad but they just said there was no such thing as ghosts, but I knew there was something. After a while it began to scare me, I mean what if there was a ghost, would it hurt me?

I became very sleepless at night, afraid to close my eyes. Then one day Mum and Dad went to a party, I begged them not to leave me, they just said, 'Stop being such a baby!'

I lay awake, scared for my life, when suddenly I heard a thud. It was from downstairs. There it was again and again. I had to investigate, as I was halfway down the stairs, *thud, thud, thud.* My teeth were literally chattering. I listened very carefully to the next thud and realised it was coming from the lounge. I grabbed a frying pan off the kitchen worktop and burst into the lounge screaming, 'Put your hands up!'

My heart suddenly filled with relief. *You idiot!* I said to myself. A chain from the hanging basket had broken off and was hitting the window. I chuckled to myself, then suddenly something cold grabbed my shoulder and nobody came when I screamed.

My parents had every policeman in Leicester searching for me. I just wanted to swoop down from the attic and tell them I was right. So this is to warn you, if you ever see a ghost - *run!* Don't make the same mistake I did, or you'll be sorry.

Michael Byrne (12)

Friday Freak Outs

I walked into the kitchen for breakfast and found my mum had been crying. Her brother, my uncle, had died suddenly and we were to go to his funeral on Friday.

Friday, the day of the funeral was also the day of my sleepover with my friend Lottie. Lottie and I had a really fun time that day. This was soon spoilt when her mum phoned to say Lottie had gone missing. Local people were helping the police to search for her. That night I had trouble sleeping. Even though my window and door were shut, a cool breeze came into my bedroom. Suddenly I heard my uncle's voice, which really freaked me. Uncle whispered for me to visit the weeping willow tree in the park. 'Follow the arrow to find your friend,' he said.

Next day at the weeping willow tree, I saw the arrow was pointing to the old hut where Lottie and I often played. I rushed towards it, only to find the latch on the ground but the handle still in place that only I could open from the outside. I pulled the door open and Lottie rushed towards me from the shadows. We were both so happy to meet again. Lottie and I rushed home, safe and well, to the great delight of her parents and the police.

That night Uncle's voice came back, saying to me, 'The weeping willow will always point you in the right direction, or listen to my words carefully.'

Natasha Hookings (12)

Soulless

Once, in a land far away, lived a boy with bloodshot eyes, a black traveller's cloak flung over his back and an axe in his stomach.

Meanwhile, Ross and Calum were casting spells at everyone.

'Stupify,' shouted Alum.

'Impedamenta,' shouted Ross.

'Och, stop it,' said Alex.

The headmaster stood up shouting, 'Stop this infernal racket!'

The students were silent.

Professor Howard called, 'We're there, *silence!* Some people can't hear themselves speak on this coach.'

As the children hurried off, Calum and Ross stayed behind.

A squeaky voice said, 'Detention for both of you.'

'Yes, Professor,' they said.

That night, Calum and Ross and the whole of the school heard a long, piercing yell of pain. Ross and Calum flung themselves out of bed and ran outside. 'I wonder who it is?' they both said.

They saw Alex lying on the ground, hexed. A long tall figure stood by his body. 'Impedamenta,' he said quietly. Ross hit the wall and yelled in pain.

A red chain wrapped itself from the tip of the figure's wand around Calum's neck.

'Ackeyo wand,' Calum called. Ross' wand flew out of his hand, Calum caught it. 'Ockulous.' One jet of green light came from both wands. The tall figure yelled in pain, then fell to the floor dead.

Suddenly, another figure came across the lawn. It had a pale white face, with bloodshot eyes and an axe sticking out of his stomach. The moon disappeared and there was another yelp of pain.

Ross Lewis (9)

Whatever Next?

'I heard on the TV, Kida Castle is spooky,' said Yasmin to her sister, Sarah.

'Why didn't you say so before? It's too late now, we are here.'

They walked through the gate then out of nowhere, a black figure walked through the wall. Lots of people ran out of the room screaming, 'Ghost in there!'

'Run!' screamed Sarah.

'*No,'* said Yasmin. 'This is a good story to tell at school.'

'Come on, you two,' said Mum, who was running along with Dad.

Sarah ran after them, but Yasmin stayed behind. Under her breath she said, 'Baby.'

As Yasmin entered the room, there was nothing there. Yasmin came out of the room. She followed her mum, dad and sister, but they ran back shouting, 'The ghost again.' They told Yasmin where they saw it. She ran there.

Yasmin went inside, no one was there. Yasmin was feeling very brave. She went back to find her mum, dad and sister, but they weren't there. She heard people shouting, 'A ghost ate some people.' It was her mum, dad and sister.

Yasmin got woken up by a strange noise. It was only a dream.

Natalie Dines (9)

The Graveyard

One Tuesday night at 11pm, Barney, Kirstein, Rochelle and Nev (the blue bear) were coming home. They lived behind a graveyard. Normally they weren't scared of going through the graveyard, but this night was different. It was a full moon.

'Scared,' said Nev.

'Oh, don't be such a baby,' said Barney.

Suddenly, out of nowhere, *'Hoooowl.'*

'Run!' screamed Kirstein.

They started to run through the graveyard.

'Wooooooooo.'

'Argh, it's a ghost. Run!' screamed Barney in a girl's voice.

'Woopdeedoo,' said Rochelle, not surprised.

Then out of the shadows came a mysterious figure in a black cape and bloodsucking fangs. They ran as fast as they could.

'Argh!' screamed Kirstein, as a colony of bats came flying out from behind a gravestone.

'I'm scared,' said Nev.

'Just carry on running,' said Barney.

Finally they got home.

Bang!

'What was that?' said Nev.

'Only thunder,' said Barney.

Rochelle burst out laughing.

'What's the matter?' said Nev.

'I did all of that,' said Rochelle.

'What, everything? The thunder, ghost, spooky figure, all of it?' said Barney.

'Everything except the thunder, yes. I did it to scare you.'

The other three went to bed in a strop and had a haunted dream.

In the morning, Barney said to Nev, 'Will you go through the graveyard again?'

Nev said, 'N-n-ah!'

And they *never,* and I mean *never,* went through the graveyard again.

Roselind Hinwood (9)

Ghostbusters

'Go to sleep, darling,' said Mum.

'I will, Mum,' said Lily.

Mum closed the door and walked down the stairs. The door opened and closed and opened and closed. Lily heard footsteps coming up the stairs, they got louder and louder.

The door burst open and a monster jumped in. *'Raaa!'* the monster shouted

Lily was petrified. She got out of her bed and cuddled her toy pony called Lady. The monster came closer and closer.

'Come with me to my planet called Glaxic,' said the monster.

Lily heard a noise. She looked out of her window and she saw an army of ghosts.

Dring, dring, went the telephone. 'Hello, who is this?' said Lily in a sweet voice.

'It's the Ghostbusters!' And they hung up.

Boom! Smash! All the ghosts were gone and Lily climbed back into bed and fell fast asleep.

Kay Hamersley (9)

The Mysterious Forest

It was a regular old day; Leanne and I were walking home from school. To get home, we had to go through the forest and past the big oak tree, across the field and down the lane. We started to walk through the forest, it was quite scary but at least we had each other. When we got to the oak tree, we always knew that we had to turn left but before we did, we climbed the oak tree and looked over the forest. But we had a real shock coming our way. When we went on this afternoon, the old oak tree was nowhere to be seen, it had been cut down. So had all the other trees in the forest and there were house being built there that very minute. We decided to go into the house where the old oak tree had been.

The house was a brown thatched house. Inside it was like paradise, but it didn't smell very nice. I was in the bedroom and Leanne was in the garden, then suddenly there was a loud knock at the door. We were really scared. Then we heard the door open. We headed up the stairs and towards the bedroom. The bedroom door opened and ...

Millie Rickleton (9)

The Ghost Of All Schools

'Hello,' said a strange voice outside Joe's classroom.

'What?' Joe asked.

'Hello,' the voice said again.

Joe hid, more scared than ever. Outside, Joe heard footsteps coming towards him, then the door slowly opened and a ghost walked in.

Suddenly, the ghost said, 'I know you're in here!' and walked in further. He then added, 'Come, my allies.' Then a lot of monster ghosts rose from the ground.

Joe spotted, with horror, his friend Matt was one of them. Suddenly, they walked around the room. Luckily, Joe escaped and ran. Hurrying, he got to his other friend, Timmy, and told him. They ran together as two monsters rose from the ground and started chasing them. Then they hid in their rooms, but even though the door was locked, a ghost came through the wall of Timmy's room. It sucked the soul out of him. Now Timmy became one of them and flew off to Joe's room. Luckily for Joe, he had run off to hide with Michael. Timmy was now furious to find Joe not there and ran off to Ross' room. Ross was prepared though, he had a cross, but then he remembered that was only for vampires and was gone for sure.

Eventually the whole school suffered. So what could stop yours from being next?

Calum Mackervoy (10)

The Child With No Life

One evening, five teenagers went to a haunted house. They had once read a story about a boy who'd lost his life. The boy had been murdered outside his house. Now, the little boy haunts the murderer's house.

The next day ...

The teenagers got to the house, then they heard a loud voice shouting, 'Help me, I'm stuck.' Then the boys thought that someone was trapped, but the little boy who got killed was playing a trick on them so they would come in and the boy could suck out their life. The teenagers went in. They were shouting, 'Where are you?' The ghost flew so fast past them they did not know what it was. Then they looked behind them. They saw that one of their friends was gone.

The little boy brought the teenager into the murderer's bedroom. The little boy crept up behind him then grabbed him and sucked out his life. The ghost took the dead body and hid him.

All of the boys were really scared, then they heard the shout of the ghost saying, 'Get out, or you will die like your friend.' So the boys thought of a plan to get rid of the ghost. The teenagers got some acid and put it in a bucket. When the ghost flew down the corridor, the boys slung all of the acid on the ghost. The ghost melted slowly. They quickly drove home and the boys never went to a haunted house again.

Michael Bond (9)

The Haunted House

It was a Friday night when it happened. I'd just moved house that day. I got into bed and fell asleep straight away, but then something woke me up. It was cold (what felt like) breath! I thought it quite strange as it was midsummer and there was nobody else in the house. I went back to sleep, but was soon woken up again. Instead of a cold breeze, the lights kept turning on and off. I thought it quite scary, so I just went under the covers. But then I heard a loud, pitiful *scream!* I stayed under the cover thinking about the breeze, the lights and the scream. I scared myself to sleep.

Next time I woke up, the whole room was shaking and the door slammed shut and locked. Then a man came through the wall, hovered over me, then vanished through the wall next to me. I survived that night there, but the next day I decided to ask some questions and get some answers.

I asked the next-door neighbour to see if she knew anything about it. She said, 'There was an old man who lived there and he died suddenly, with no explanation.'

That night I did not sleep there. I moved all my belongings back to my old house. Next time I move house, I'll make sure it's not haunted. But how can I?

Olivia Gannon (10)

Untitled

I sat waiting nervously for my mother to walk through the door, she had been to parents' evening and Mr Brooke didn't like me much. The clock struck six and the doorbell rang. I answered and a mailman stood at the door with his fluorescent red cap, he stood with a huge parcel up to his chest with my mum's name stamped on the top.

The clock struck ten, Mum was still out, what could have happened to her? I went straight up to bed, as my foot touched the soft step, the parcel shook, I ran upstairs and covered myself with the blanket, within time I fell to sleep.

My alarm clock woke me up at seven in the morning, I got ready for school and ran into my mother's room, I pounced on her duvet and she wasn't there, the smell of washing-up liquid filled my nose with delight. Just then the front door slammed shut, the delight turned to a rotting smell, I pushed myself off the bed and ran downstairs. I went to grab my shoes, however they weren't there, they were hovering in the front room, I grabbed them and ran to my grandad's house.

My grandad explained that it must have been my great grandad, and that he'd be doing it, he'd been doing it for 10 years. I questioned 'But that doesn't explain the parcel!'

Rebecca Finnie (13)
Bigwood School, Business & Enterprise College, Nottingham

The Silhouette In The Water

It was a dark, gloomy night and me and my friends were in the sitting room in our hotel. We had a few weeks off from college and decided to take a holiday to Spain, the hotel was nice but the pool was rather gloomy. Me and my friends were deciding what to do that night. We all decided to go where we liked and meet near the pool.

1am, we all met up at the pool. Suddenly there was a loud *splash!* We looked to see what was happening, there was nothing. I pointed out a silhouette in the water, it was a human silhouette. We ignored it, it could have been the pattern on the pool floor. We went to our rooms.

The next night, it happened again, we ignored it again. It happened the next night, we couldn't ignore it anymore. The next night something different happened, the silhouette rose out of the water. It looked so delicate and real, but unreal at the same time. The silhouette stared at my friend, she stared back and began walking towards it. We screamed at her to come back but it was like she couldn't hear us. And, before we could stop her, she had walked into the pool holding the silhouette's hand.

She went under, we screamed at her. We ran through the water, we could see her struggling but as we got there, she floated back up. She had drowned.

Rochelle Freestone-McDonald (14)
Bigwood School, Business & Enterprise College, Nottingham

The Cry Of Death

The misty, shallow grave, stood up like a brave soldier. As the frail, old man, who had a very faint sight was viewing cautiously. Bats flew overhead, squawking fiercely. A silhouette appeared vaguely, barely visible. The old man stumbled over a tree root, the silhouette came closer. 'Stay back, I'm warning you,' the old man cried impatiently. The smell of tar and blood was wafted into the man's nose. The silhouette reached into his pocket, the watch was placed in front of the man. The trance proceeded, he followed everything the stranger said.

The old man gazed completely helpless of the surroundings around him. Although wherever he looked, he viewed a river of blood, dark red blood. His feet started moving helplessly, the man cried in fear but nothing came out, not even a squeak.

The shallow chamber room, the man now stood in had no character. Just a stone-grey room and a breezy draft from the cracks in the wall. Shrieks and screams came from the room above, the man now knew it was the Cry of Death. Was he next? The cold sweat dribbled down his neck.

The silhouette stood in the doorway again with a strange mask covering his face. With one swipe, not even enough time for a gasp of air, the man was dead.

You never know, the silhouette may be out there waiting for the next victim.

Stephen Landon (12)
Bigwood School, Business & Enterprise College, Nottingham

Two Of A Kind

My name is Karl and I roam the Earth looking for my killer. I died in 1897 September 1st, I remember that day like it was yesterday.

It was a cold, dark night, I was hiking through the woods when I felt I sharp pain in the bottom of my back. I fell to the ground when a man whispered into my ear. 'Say goodbye to life.' He put a gun to my head and pulled the trigger.

'Help me!' they were my last breaths, my last words.

I now search for him, the monster who killed me, I try to remember which way he went but I never quite saw, but today I flew into a great, big, mossy grey gate. I flew up and up to the top and there was a scary, haunted house. I went over to the door which was covered in cobwebs, then all of a sudden, a man opened the door, there stood my killer. I ran away as fast as I could, he was there in front of me, I had to go back there.

I went in the middle of the night. I walked into the house, it felt cold and lonely. It felt as if no one lived there. I walked up to his room. I grabbed a pillow and put it over the rotten, evil, cowardly face. Then his face came through it. He was a ghost!

Vikki Allen (13)
Bigwood School, Business & Enterprise College, Nottingham

I Dare You ...

'I dare you ...'

Dare me to do what? I thought. Practical jokes I can handle them, like a laugh as much as the next person but this? This is insane. It had been going on for ages, about two months. Nobody knew what was going on. Who was this person that tortured my dreams? Snapping out of my trance, I realised where I was.

The house.

The place where Reggie had been ... murdered. The day replayed in my head as I stared at the house. I remember seeing people milling around, me running past them. The stench smothered me like a blanket choking me. The kitchen was the worst, glass was everywhere but on the walls, three words ...

I dare you ... and then I realised it all started when Reggie died. Something moved. Glancing up I saw an eerie light disappearing in the window.

I froze ... somehow I ran, what was happening?

3 days later in the paper, boy of 13 found dead. Doctors baffled.

The family have moved into the house, settling fine, with them is a boy of 13, he is alone. Out of the corner of his eye he sees an eerie light disappearing and three words are etched in the wall.

I dare you.

Chantelle Green (12)
Bigwood School, Business & Enterprise College, Nottingham

Ghost Story

With a groan of annoyance, the smartly dressed man descended from the driver's seat. He peered through the thick fog at the smoking engine, and realising little could be done at this late hour, he was relieved to see a neon motel sign looking at him from the shadows.

The receptionist was an elderly lady with a ghostly pallor. However as he walked towards the rotting stairs, he heard a gravely voice say, 'Beware of mysterious phone calls.' Whirling round in surprise he looked at the wrinkled lady, who in turn gazed back at him innocently.

Dismissing the incident from his mind, he found his room and slipped beneath the covers.

Drifting into an uneasy sleep, the man awoke in the small hours of the morning to the sound of a ringing telephone; he picked up the receiver and heard only a deep woman's laugh along with the warning. 'Leave now or pay the forfeit.'

He was certain this was merely a prank call, and frustrated the man flicked the switch and was plunged into darkness once more.

He awoke with the rays of the sun streaming intermittently through the blinds, and he scrambled out of bed, remembering he was expected at a meeting later that day.

Reaching the car, the man turned the ignition key, momentarily forgetting about his breakdown the previous night. He was therefore astonished when the car began first time, and smiling at his good fortune, he turned the tuner on the radio. The only sound that filled the car was the deep laugh of a woman.

Charlotte Blick (14)
Bryanston School, Blandford

Ghost Story

The boy had been happily chasing butterflies with the sun beating down on him. He felt his foot catch on something, something covered his face. It smelt sweet. His body felt limp. Everything went black.

Years later you could still feel the terror in the field, despite the heat of the summer's day, the air was void of sound, not even leaves rustling in the wind. Locals knew not to walk in these parts so the man walking his dog must have been new to the village.

As the man walked along a path that ran alongside the wood at the edge of the field, he looked at ease but his dog did not, the dog was behind the man, as if it were hiding from something. About halfway around the field, the dog suddenly stopped and lay on the floor whining. The owner tugged on its lead but the dog just wouldn't budge.

The dog started to growl, at one point there was an eerie child's laugh from further up the field, the man spun around, out of the corner of his eye, he thought he saw a small child but he must have been imagining it, as he only saw it in a split-second.

Moving his attention back to the dog, the man saw that the dog was on its side and blood was trickling from its mouth, someone or something had just killed his dog. The laughter started again but this time it was clearer. Looking around the man saw a ghostly figure of a child chasing butterflies. The figure only stayed for a second and then vanished once again. A shadow enveloped the man and he dropped to the ground.

A couple of days later, the farmer was checking his crop when he saw the body of a young man, encrusted with blood. The man was holding a dog lead with a dog collar on the end but no dog.

The farmer heard an eerie laugh from the woods. His time had come.

Tom Frew (15)
Bryanston School, Blandford

Mud Mounds

Mersey is a small woodland village in Wiltshire, famous for supposedly having a ghost in the town that is out to kill young children. There are only two children living in the village at the moment. Lucy and Anne, 6-year-old twins. They enjoy exploring the woods and climbing trees.

It was a dark and stormy autumn night in Mersey and the following morning, the two girls went out into the woods to see what damage had been done to the trees. All the leaves had been blown off the trees and there was the odd big branch that had fallen off. The girls were walking through the woods when they came across a circular opening where there were no leaves in the middle, there was a small mound of fresh earth. The girls thought this was a bit odd but they went and investigated anyway, as they approached the mound, they noticed quite a strong and disgusting smell. The girls stood by the mound and discussed whether to dig it up or not. They decided to dig the earth away and see what was underneath it.

The smell got stronger as they dug with hands removing the damp soil. Lucy put her hand under the soil when she felt something, she tried pulling it out but it wouldn't move, the object was cold and rigid. She moved the soil away that covered the object. 'It's a hand!' Lucy shouted. The girls both let out a deafening scream that everyone in the village heard.

The villagers ran out into the woods and began searching for the little girls. The girl's father came across a circular opening, where there were no leaves and in the middle, he saw three mounds of fresh earth.

Ed Allison (15)
Bryanston School, Blandford

The Clown

One dark, misty night, the doorbell sounded and the parents opened the door onto the babysitter. They greeted her and then immediately the parents departed the house and the babysitter took over. The babysitter put the children to bed straight away, tucking them up and turning the lights off.

The babysitter disappeared downstairs and started searching for food and a drink and found a comfortable room downstairs. After she had had a fair amount of food and started to become bored, she decided to look around the house, which was big with many rooms.

Her experience of looking round had not enlightened her, to be honest, far from it, the rooms were big, blank and over spacious and the size of the house had suddenly dawned on her, being the only person awake in the building. Also to her disappointment, she had not discovered a TV, so she gave herself the task of finding the TV to keep her occupied. She began to journey upstairs.

On her way peculiar surreal shadows formed on the wall, everything went silent but she still carried on up thinking it was nothing. It was only after she entered the large room, which she guessed was the parents' room, shivers were sent down her spine and everything became cold as she saw the clown statue staring at her through icy eyes. On the plus, she had found the TV but felt guilty for not asking the parents. She paced down the stairs, out of pure fear and picked up the phone, they answered immediately and she began to ask, 'Do you think I can use the TV and do you mind if I cover the clown's statue's face up as it is rather spooky?'

He replied, 'What clown statue?'

Alec Renton (15)
Bryanston School, Blandford

The Honourable

It was like any other Thursday for Lizzie, little did she know that as soon as she stepped foot inside the house, everything would change. Today she had woken up with a strange feeling, she couldn't place and as the day progressed it grew stronger.

She walked into her kitchen later that day and found that someone was already there. 'Who, who are you?' she spluttered. The figure looked at her blankly, it was a girl of about her age, with blonde hair and bright blue eyes.

'Hello Lizzie, I've been waiting for you,' murmured the girl, 'I've been waiting for so long, and you don't even remember me!' she let out a short quiet laugh.

'Who are you? Why are you in my house?' asked Lizzie quietly, fear engulfing her body.

'Don't you remember me you silly girl! It's Jane! Your invisible friend who you abandoned when you were eight years old! Well I'm no so invisible anymore am I, and now I'm going to take over your life and abandon you, you see how it feels!' Then everything went black, and Lizzie was not Lizzie anymore; she was nothing.

You see the strange thing was no one noticed that everything had changed about Lizzie Jones that day. They didn't notice how her hair colour had changed, even her laugh. Everyone who had loved Lizzie didn't realise. Even when her mother arrived ten minutes later she didn't even realise that the face of her child had changed. She didn't realise that the real Lizzie was still there, just invisible, living in a twisted nightmare that wouldn't stop until she managed to find a way out. For now anyway Jane would live her life, there wasn't anything she could do to stop her.

Grace Cavanagh-Butler (14)
Bryanston School, Blandford

Sleep

Sleep. Dreams. These are what we need to be human. Insomnia. Nightmares. These are products of the human mind. When does the human turn from sleep to insomnia? From dreams to nightmares?

The room. Dark. Too dark. Not a sound. The silence screamed. Paranoia. Fear. I felt something … sinister. My heart. Stopped. Cold as ice. Pouring out of me. Sweat. My muscles tightened. The presence slithered all around me. I rose. Walking to the door. The handle, twisted around my hand. Like a snake. I recoiled. I fought instinct. I tore open the door. Nothing. The moon shone through the skylight. Eerie, the walls, shivered. My eyes focused on the placid hallway. It flashed past. The walls rippled. Pictures crumpled. Smashed. Then silence. As I followed it. The carpet bore a glass coating. Tearing flesh. Soaking my feet in a warm blanket. Bloodiest footprints. Following a chaotic path. I walked. The darkness downstairs. No light. No sound. I reached the bottom … and fell. My face. Met, not floor. But splintered wood. Again warmth. In a cold room. I was enticed into the kitchen. Felt warmth. Flowing out of my body. On the tile floor. A figure stood over me. In his presence. Felt warmth. Flowing out of my body. Something cold in my chest. From the face. A bloodiest mouth. Dripping over mine. A searing pain. My icy body. I realised. Not a nightmare. Not asleep …

Edward Godfrey (14)
Bryanston School, Blandford

Faint Outlines

From that moment I knew my fate. The looks in our eyes; evil in his and terror in mine. 'It's over Melanie; it's too late to change what you did to me. You ruined our lives and it's time you pay!' As I stood, backed up against the cold, moist stones; a tear trickled down my face but my arms too rigid with fear to wipe it away. As my life flashed before my eyes, knife to my throat, I began to think about had caused this malicious act; was I that bad?

On that dull morning, no longer than a week ago, I awoke with a jump as I came round from a terrible dream, the same as the previous nights. I chuckled to myself about how childish it was, but could this mean something? My father died years ago. I'm safe from him now. As I turned around, in front of me stood an old man; but there was something different. This was only a faint outline. Stronger than yesterday, but still faint.

As he came towards me, I saw the hatred of his eyes. My father had never loved me. I had always known that I was an accident and my parents wished I wasn't alive, but before had I been this threatened by him. He came closer and closer, step by step, and I realised if I didn't get out soon I might never. I cowered away from him towards the stone wall.

Jessie Reynolds (14)
Bryanston School, Blandford

Frozen Section

I was asked by Mother to go to the corner shop for milk, so reluctantly, I took the money from my mother's hand.

I strolled out of the door, to the back gate. I dragged my feet while walking.

I got to the shop, which was named after this weird old man who lived next door in the shop I walked over to the cold meat section, looked around, and this was the first time I had looked round the shop that evening and I realised that there was no one around, no one buying anything and no one behind the counter.

I looked again at frozen food and realised the sticky slippery surface I was standing on, I looked down half-heartedly and noticed the red floor. I looked towards the counter and I became aware of where the red on the floor had come from, an arm lay limp on the counter.

I suddenly noticed a shadow behind me. I turned briskly to a man with a little muscle beside his left eye twitching madly and he had a shiny object in his right hand which I dared not look at. But I couldn't help but glance and I dreaded it, that moment I realised it was a gun.

I looked around to where the arm was and saw the person's face, which was drenched on a red sheet of blood and a black hole in the middle of his forehead.

Then I saw the man with the gun leave the shop.

Tabitha Evans (15)
Bryanston School, Blandford

Untitled

One day in June at dusk a member of the school office suddenly comes bursting through the door. She tells me that they have just got a phone call from someone with no name saying that they need me to go home immediately and that there is a pre-paid taxi waiting for me outside.

As I walk out of the school building towards the taxi, I am thinking *why is this happening? Has something gone wrong? Has one of my relatives died? Has someone played a prank? Where may I be going? Why would I be going to this place?* Once I was in the taxi going to my destination, I am thinking of talking to the driver who seems like a stranger. Anyway the journey seems to be going rather quickly, may be too quickly but that is not bothering me. What is though, is that I am shaking and I feel worried.

Once the journey is over, I get out, walk up the door, try pushing through, I go to find, to my horror, inside is the man that must have phoned and I know that this is not good.

I am right, I now know this is not good because the man in front of me is a ghost. He gets a knife from the kitchen, comes back, slices at me and connects. I see him disappear as I fall to the floor and pass away.

Augustus Persson (15)
Bryanston School, Blandford

Knock, Knock, Who's There?

Knock, knock. I woke from my deep sleep. *Knock, knock.* As I awoke, I slowly started to realise that there was someone at the door. I glanced at my watch, 10.30am. Must be the postman. I heard the *knock, knock* again and I realised that this was not the postman; must be a neighbour.

I drowsily walked downstairs and towards the door, *knock, knock*. 'Coming.' I now fastened my pace realising that whoever was at the door, wanted my answer quickly.

I reached forward and turned the door handle. *Swush.* A gust of wind slammed the door open, nearly knocking me over. I regained my senses and looked outside, there was no one there, just the sun shining on my face. This however did strike me as odd, where had that gust of wind come from? But as I had told my daughter on many occasions, life is full of things we can't explain.

I was about to shut the door, then I heard the knocking again. *Knock, knock, knock.* This time it was at the back door and it sounded as if it was being broken down. I ran to the back door hoping to capture the culprit, but as before I was only greeted with a gust of wind. I slammed the door. Then I heard an agonising scream. I ran upstairs into my daughter's room. As I burst in I felt a strong gust of wind and turning towards her bed, saw my worst fear.

Julian Sebag-Montefiore (15)
Bryanston School, Blandford

From History To Misery

Waiting for the bell to ring, I stare out the frosty window; everything is so deadly silent. Suddenly, I snap out of it. I can hear faint footsteps coming from the corridor. They get louder and louder and quicker and quicker. They're coming towards my classroom. The door is pushed open and Mrs Dent, the school secretary, hurries through it. Breathless, she pauses a moment, staring at a class of speechless pupils waiting for her to say something. She whispers something to the teacher and a look of horror is painted on his face. He tells us to go wait outside. We reluctantly leave our desks and crowd outside the classroom.

In the corridor, Sophie presses her ear against the cold steel door and says slowly, 'They're talking about the back corridor, there's something there. Let's go see.' Stupidly we all follow her out of the main corridor and up a little staircase at the back of the building. We all stumble into the back corridor and the squeaky door slams behind us. Looking around us, I suddenly notice that everyone is staring at the ground in horror. I push my way to the front and see a knife, drenched in blood, with a pool of dark red blood next to it. A few metres away lies a young boy. He does not seem alive.

Two nurses come running round the corner, I turn around and at the other end of the corridor, I watch a shadow run away into the darkness.

Chloë Stonex-Bonnet (14)
Bryanston School, Blandford

Untitled

James was waiting for his mum to pick him up. He felt a curious sensation of being watched. Five minutes later, she turned up and he jumped in the car. He still felt this curious sensation of being watched.

He arrived home and continued to feel this probing feeling. Later on, the feeling became more intense. It felt like something was writhing through his veins. His mum said he seemed pale and withdrawn. He tried to enlighten her on this physical trauma but words did not seem to clarify the strange feeling.

Later he felt nauseous, he told his parents that he was going to sleep. His sleep was erratic, he often woke up, and at times during this night, he felt a strange feeling of something being drawn out of him.

Sometime in the early hours, he woke up with this same feeling only more intense, he felt sick, he rushed to his bathroom, he splashed his face with water but he felt the same. The feelings reached a peak and he felt things coming out of about where his navel is, strange shimmering shapes darted in the room, a hypnotic movement, like those of humans. He felt he was going to pass out. The shapes had peculiar human appearances, they had facial expressions. Eventually he closed his eyes and went to sleep one last time.

Benedict Bell (15)
Bryanston School, Blandford

Daisy

With a start I came to, I tried to move but I couldn't. I felt drowsy and weak. I looked up to see an iridescent white couch. *Where am I? How did I get here?* I thought. The last thing I knew I was walking home from school. Mother's probably worried sick. There was a dirty window, which was frosted up with ice. *That's odd,* I thought, *we've never had snow in summer!* My legs were stiff and sore, my muscles felt abandoned. I looked down to see bruises all over my legs. How long had I been in here? The light was droning on and off and there was not another sound but faint footsteps in the distance.

I heard a man approach the room. He was talking to someone else, explaining something and I could hear the faint voice of a woman, she didn't sound happy. There was something familiar about the woman's voice but I couldn't quite make it out. They walked in. It was Mother! (With a man I didn't recognise.)

'How odd, look at that window darling, it's all frosted up,' the man shivered.

The woman began to cry. 'I'm sorry, it's just, it smells of Daisy in here, I miss her.'

It was only then I realised they couldn't see me.

Georgie Boothman (15)
Bryanston School, Blandford

Creep

Miles couldn't quite figure it out. A faint creaking sound, eerily travelling from one end of the dark corridor to the other. In such a large house, strange noises were common. However, there was something distinct about this one, something unnatural, as if the floor was creaking in fear at the presence of something or someone approaching. He couldn't help thinking that something was wrong. What puzzled Miles was the fact that the alarm hadn't sounded? Surely that would have made Miles feel better, but no, he was still unsettled. He traipsed back towards the end of the dimly lit corridor.

Another thing that made Miles feel uneasy was the darkness at the end of the corridor. It was never normally so dark, even in winter. He put it from his mind reminding himself of the late hour, 3 o'clock he made it.

As he walked through the door there was a loud crack which scared the life out of him, he jumped and swivelled round. There was a wave of cold air coursing through him and all around him. The corridor seemed to glow an odd colour, he swore he could see a figure. This time he ran. He ran through the ancient house, passing rooms full of portraits of his disapproving ancestors, up to his room on the top floor, and slammed the door.

As he sat there, heart pounding, mind racing, his fear turned to horror. He became aware of a malevolent presence all around him.

Lyle Somerset (15)
Bryanston School, Blandford

Ghost Story

It was my entire fault my brother was dead, I had killed him! My mind always changes, one minute I'm fine, and the next I'm not. It's like someone else is inside me, taking over me. My hands were smeared with his blood, dripping and flowing onto the floor.

I scrunched down into a deep, darkened corner and sobbed my heart out. I stared into the gloomy distance; I had a vision of my brother, which stuck so strong in my mind staring at me, his eyes looked frozen, dead. I couldn't handle it! *What have I done?*

I felt a cold shiver run down my back, I could feel someone was right behind me grabbing hold of my arms. I knew he had come back, he had come for me! I turned around shivering with fear. I saw my brother in the corner of my eye, bleeding and crying and I went to help him but I couldn't move, I went to talk to him but my lips wouldn't move. His cries echoed through the walls, his tears drowned the floor. His heart was dead but his spirit was still alive. The walls steamed up, the light flickered.

I couldn't do anything about it, he was dead and it was my fault, I would never forgive myself, not even God could forgive me. I could feel his presence with me, next to me! My heart pounded so hard, I couldn't breathe, someone had grabbed around my neck, it was him ...

Maddy Smedley (13)
Dartford Grammar School for Girls, Dartford

Beast In The Darkness

A blood-curdling scream pierced through the darkness of the dungeon. Emma heard the deafening roar and froze. She was sure the beast could hear her heart beating. The wild thumping under her vest was surely enough to give her hiding place away. After all, the beast was attracted to live flesh and blood.

She crouched on the slippery, bloodstained floor. Emma wanted to cry, but panic and shock had paralysed her. Silence. Suddenly the beast's footsteps echoed through the tunnel, nearer and nearer at a supernatural speed. It had found her! Emma ran for her life.

Fear blinded her. The creature had her now, its clawed grasp inches away from her skin; closer and closer. Emma closed her eyes, and collapsed into a sticky puddle. There was a skull near her face, its empty sockets leering at her out of the darkness.

A fierce wind surrounded her as the creature sniffed and exhaled foul-smelling breath over her body. Emma waited for the killer blow to her neck but it never came. Slowly, she raised her head and stared into the beast's eyes. They glowed red, yellow, poisonous blue, a vivid purple, and then a deadly and venomous green.

Emma realised she had been tricked. The creature liked its prey to suffer before dying. She knew that her death would be slow and painful. Suddenly the monster lunged, its teeth bared into a grotesque grin. For the first time since entering the dark tunnels, Emma screamed.

Sophie Snow (13)
Dartford Grammar School for Girls, Dartford

The Wind

Her long black hair flowed across her cold, pale face. She lay there, her lifeless body glowing paler in the moonlight. The trees around her swayed as the wind blew them softly. But there was a silence that not even the rummaging of the trees could break. The dagger, which had been buried deep into her heart, was still there, the killer hadn't even had the courtesy to remove the weapon. He wasn't even a known killer like the ones on the wanted posters but he had personal reasons for this kill and although he hadn't been experienced he had managed to frame someone else.

But lurking in the shadows was something greater and so much more powerful that anyone should be terrified of. His eyes glinted like the stars in the moonlight. His claws grasped the air around her sucking her in. The leaves around her started to swirl and its claws came closer as she heard its icy but heavy breath creep up. It tore and shredded her limb from limb. Her blood trickled down her stone-cold body, her eyes bulged as she was ripped and devoured. She was caught on the unlucky night in November, on which one member of Dartford was devoured every year.

Sarah Tuffley (13)
Dartford Grammar School for Girls, Dartford

The Mysterious Ghosts

The trees and bushes were screaming in the storm. The lights in the houses were flickering on and off. I tried running back to my house as quickly as possible but the path seemed never-ending. My heart was beating faster by the second. Reaching a clump of trees, I took shelter behind a tree trunk to catch my breath. I started running again to get to safety but felt something on my shoulder. It stopped me. I turned around and there was a transparent person standing right in front of me. I was amazed and couldn't believe it, what was it? Before I could even think anything, it dragged me and took me into a house.

When I entered, I saw many more transparent people. They were ghosts! I asked the ghost why it had brought me here but it didn't reply. All the ghosts smiled but none of them actually spoke to me. I couldn't understand what was happening.

They pulled me along, this time making me fly. I was so confused. They took me from one room to another. The rooms kept getting smaller one by one. When I entered the last room, there was a ghost sitting on a chair but he was huge, hundred times bigger than the other ones. He held out a box, picked me up, put me inside it and then …

Sonal Wadhwani (13)
Dartford Grammar School for Girls, Dartford

1968

1968 - A little girl called Amy was playing catch in the park, until her friends accidentally threw the ball into an abandoned house. Amy, being kind, offered to go get it but only if her friend watched her. She stepped into the garden, slowly approached the door holding her favourite dolly, singing a song her dead mother taught her. 'I am a big girl, I am a big girl, I am strong, I am strong because Mummy takes care of me all day long, all day long.'

She reached the door, pushed the door open and stepped into the house. The door slammed shut. Inside the house was pitch-black. Out of nowhere a lit candle appeared.

'Argh!' That is all the girls outside heard ...

2006 - 38 years later people went to knock down the abandoned house and saw a dead little girl holding her dolly with a lit candle beside her. They were suspicious about it but before they could call anyone the girl pulled out a knife and stabbed them to death then set the house alight. Everything burst into flames, but she walked out perfectly fine with an innocent smile on her face.

Later that day a little girl went to visit a lady. The girl asked, 'Have you lived here since 1968?'

She replied, 'Yes.'

The girl began to sing, 'I am a big girl, I am strong, you're a gonna when I finish this song ...'

'Argh!' that's all that was heard.

Mark Kaliisa (14)
Deptford Green School, London

Beware Of The Warehouse

Nicky and Grace stood staring in the moonlight at the derelict building that stood before them. They wondered how they would ever live this down if they didn't complete this dare.

Nicky crept up to the rusty door at the front of the warehouse, she pushed it slightly and a cloud of dust filled the air.

Grace walked up to a crack in the wall over to the right of the building and squeezed through it, Nicky followed rather uncomfortably.

The warehouse was filled with dust and abandoned pushchairs, trolleys, sofas and much more. Nicky picked her way through all the mess and caught up with Grace who was peering around her.

Nicky linked on to Grace's arm and told her how much she was dreading venturing into the warehouse.

Suddenly there was a voice, it echoed around the building.

'Grace, did you hear that?' asked Nicky.

'Yes,' Grace replied.

'Who was it do you think?'

'I don't know Nicky, but it definitely wasn't me.'

The voice came again but this time louder.

'Kill!'

'Grace I want to go.'

'No, we have to do this ... we have to.'

'I'm scared.'

'How will we ever live this down if we don't complete it?' asked Grace.

'We won't,' replied Nicky.

'Argh!'

'Nicky, shut up.'

'I'm so scared, I want to go.'

There was a flash of light and Grace fell to her knees.

'Grace!' Nicky cried.

Grace had stopped breathing and lay dead in the dust ...

Meghan Bradley (12)
English Martyrs School, Leicester

The Death House

There once was a house which people said was haunted by a man who died there. When the police found him, they could barely recognise him because he was covered in blood and only half of him was left.

There was a boy who wanted to go in the house but he wasn't allowed to (of course). One day he was playing out with his friends when they came to the house. It was grey and dull with fungus growing off of it ... it was disgusting, but John liked it.

John said to his friends, 'Let's go in,' his friends were like him, they found disgusting things good. They agreed to go in. Before he touched the door, it creaked slowly open like the groan of an old man.

The floor was as soggy as a sponge, the whole house was covered in spiderwebs. They all started to walk into the front room, and Timmy was at the back and the door slammed shut. Timmy turned round and when he turned back ... 'Argh!' Everyone looked back, but no one could see him...

Jamie Roberts (12)
English Martyrs School, Leicester

The Drip In The Night

It was dark, there was no light, everybody was asleep, when from the sky there was a *drip, drip, drip!* Jesse woke up and looked out of the window, nothing, so he went back to sleep. Later, *drip, drip, drip*. He woke, looked out. Nothing. So he went back to sleep. But then *drip, drip, drip.* He woke, looked out and there were droplets of red on his window. His heartbeat picked up. *Drip, drip, drip*. He screamed and ran into his parent's bedroom. *Drip, drip, drip*. He peered out the window, no red droplets. He was being silly.

He got back into bed and went back to sleep. But *drip, drip, drip.* He had to get away so he ran downstairs and into the garden. He was just out of the door when something wet fell on his shoulder. He looked and there was a red spot on his pyjamas. He ran down to the bottom of the garden and looked up onto the roof. There, pierced by the satellite, was his uncle who had died the previous week. He screamed as three drips of blood fell from the body, *drip, drip, drip.*

From that day on, through every night and every day, they could hear the taunting drips of blood falling from the body. *Drip, drip, drip.*

Helen Picken (12)
English Martyrs School, Leicester

Screaming Doom

The bleak, cold wind swept across the dusty street, in a mysterious way. A small abnormal boy staggered through an alleyway, raiding out of a dustbin, searching for food.

Then he heard a thunderous scream in the factory next to him and tiptoed to the entrance. Finally he broke the chain of the door and slowly entered the spooky factory.

He steadily turned on the lights and curiously stepped along. The sound of terror rushed through the atmosphere. Suddenly the boy sprinted to the source of this mystery. His eyes gazed upon a cold-blooded killer, who was grasping a sharp, long, bulky axe that was dripping in blood.

On the floor was a dead figure, the boy saw the beastly murderer smirk. The truth was uncovered, that it was the boy's mother, who had recently found out she was pregnant.

One lives ... and one dies.

Emily Winterton (12)
English Martyrs School, Leicester

The Ghost In The Manor House

One Tuesday in Nottingham it was pouring down with rain. There lived a girl called Amethyst. She lived on 1234 Hungrington Drive. At the bottom of her garden was the start of Hungrington Forest. You're not supposed to go in the forest but Amethyst was curious. She wanted to know what it looked like through the trees. There were deep, dark drops of 100ft. Got to be careful or …

'Whowwwwww,' screeched Amethyst. 'I fell down after I was so careful.' She carried on walking in the heavy downpour. She noticed a silhouette in the distance, it looked like an old manor house.

Amethyst wandered inside. The doors were creaky, the stairs were rotten, the windows were boarded up, what a tatty old place! As she carefully walked upstairs, she noticed an open bedroom door. It had 'Damien's Room' written on it. She went in. There was an old mattress on the floor. Amethyst lay down and fell asleep.

She was woken by strange noises. It scared her so much she jumped up in fright. It must have been the ghost of Damien that she had been told about by her mum. She ran downstairs and out of the house. She sped home as fast as her legs would take her. Amethyst *never* went in the forest again!

Laura Slater (11)
English Martyrs School, Leicester

How I Died

One day, Robert, a 34-year-old, black-haired cryptologist, walked into an abandoned cottage looking for work. It was creaky and, to Robert's dismay, had blood splattered everywhere. Robert pressed his finger to the blood, it wasn't fresh.

Robert pulled his Kodak from his tweed jacket and put the flash on, he took some pictures. On the picture of the blood splattered stained glass window of Jesus, his face was shrouded by another one. That of a boy. When Robert turned to the window, he was there. The boy spoke to him:

'Hello my name is Drake ... I was eaten alive and if you sit and listen, I'll tell you about it.'

Robert thought the boy looked harmless, so he sat down.

'It was a brisk day, I walked up the hill and came into here. He was here, the deranged lunatic man who needed to be put into an asylum was. He was eating a lung. Human. He didn't turn around until I slipped. He turned around, blood pouring from his mouth. I staggered back and he chased me and I could feel his eyes searing into the back of my young head.

I started throwing things at him, then a brick, it missed. He started chasing faster, the eyes searing deeper. He eventually got me and started eating me alive. First my eyes, then my major organs.'

Robert asked who the guy was.

Drake's face distorted from calm to extremely worried.

Someone shouted, 'Me!'

Robert shuffled around, the deranged lunatic man struck again. He ate Robert alive.

Emilio Zarcone (12)
English Martyrs School, Leicester

The Pictures Of Death

Walking to work one fine day, Jack found an interesting book. He tucked it under his arm. Later that day he returned to his comfortable apartment and remembering the strange book, he glanced through its colourful pages. He came across an old and interesting map. Interrupting his friend Dennis, he excitedly showed him the intriguing document. Dennis, not happy at being disturbed, finally discussed the island.

Dennis never wanted to go but Jack said if they took pictures, it would make them a lot of money. The following week, they crossed the Pacific.

A month later, they finally got off the soggy brown boat to step onto a rocky surface. They both looked up high at the massive jungle where broken leaves and rotten apples dropped onto the damp soil. Walking through the dense jungle, they heard a very loud rumbling noise. Under their feet, massive caterpillars came crawling. They pushed them off and ran at the speed of light. The giant caterpillars were right behind them, shooting poisonous thorns.

While they were running, Jack took pictures with a camera. They came to a different part of the island there was another rumbling noise making the whole island shake. More terrifying creatures came. Jack and Dennis ran for their lives, climbing a massive tree, they watched the strange creatures run past. They eventually followed the path back to the boat and returned to New York. Later Jack and Dennis showed the pictures at a party. The next day the police found their dead bodies holding the strange pictures.

Samuel Merritt (12)
Fort Hill Community School, Basingstoke

The Boy Who Never Came Back!

It was sunrise in the spike-like cornfield as the 2 lost boys dug their way to the other side. They came upon a huge, mouldy, old shack that looked 500 years old, they were going to go in but Thomas, the youngest, was so terrified that he wet himself and refused to go in, so they walked home fast.

But Ross was curious, so that night when everyone was asleep, he tiptoed out of the house, through the cornfield towards the rickety house.

As he approached it, he saw a figure go past, he pushed the door open and it creaked like broken floorboards. He went inside and a massive rat ran across the thick, deep, dust-covered carpet. Suddenly, the door slammed behind him and he screamed with horror as a massive silhouette of a hand grabbed his leg and pulled him underground.

The funny thing was, the next morning his mum and dad were looking for him everywhere but his brother knew where he was but didn't dare tell anyone in case he lost them as well!

Wendy Smith (12)
Fort Hill Community School, Basingstoke

Any One For Tennis?

The abandoned tennis court neglected with weeds, looked desolate when Dave arrived. He was scared.

'Helloo!' shouted Dave at the top of his voice, hoping that someone heard. A moment. He waited. *Bang!*

'Argh!' he screamed. 'That was strange,' he whispered quietly. He moved step by step. Making his way over to the changing rooms, he heard something in the distance. Running into the changing rooms, to his surprise, he saw a young girl in her twenties sitting, waiting on the bench opposite.

'Hello,' he said, with a worried tone in his voice.

'Hi,' she said.

'Are you waiting for anyone?' he questioned.

'Yes,' she exclaimed.

'Who?'

'The ghost of the best tennis player in England!' she said laughing.

Dave walked over to her and sat down. 'Why what happened?' he asked.

'Do you want to know the whole story?'

'Go on then,' he said.

'Well it was a cold, windy afternoon. He had just finished playing a tennis match. He went to have a shower and that was when he saw it. There it was just standing there. He didn't realise it at first but it seemed to be moving closer to him. Grabbing the towel he ran. He stopped realising that there was a strange noise coming from what appeared to be a ghost. But despite this, he carried on running. He came out to find that his girlfriend had gone. He looked everywhere but she was nowhere to be seen. He came to us and told us the story. He later died after seeing his girlfriend as a ghost,' she explained.

'I hopo that doesn't happen to me one day.'

Jemma Holmes (12)
Fort Hill Community School, Basingstoke

Now I Tell The Tale

I was on my way to my aunt's funeral with my mum and dad, boarding the train I thought, *why did she have to live so far away?* I hated going on trains, they're always so boring but what I didn't know was that all was about to change.

I gazed out of the window and stared at the blinding moonlight peeping through the dark wispy clouds. Dad had fallen asleep as usual and Mum was reading her book. I was so bored, I wished something would happen. Then suddenly the train wheels screeched along the broken track. The train came to a halt. I could see the fear in my mother's eyes, it was there until the lights went out! Everyone was panicking, women and children were screaming, Dad woke up and began to panic, but I remained seated, motionless, staring at the moon. People soon settled down, now all we could hear were the distant screams of the train driver. Dad thought it was all a joke but I knew something was wrong. My dad had had enough and went to the engine room to see what was happening. 'Do you think Dad's alright?' I asked. Mum didn't answer. I repeated my question but this time, she didn't need to answer, the screams of my father answered my question.

Two women stood up and slowly walked along the narrow corridor looking for their brother. They slipped over, when they realised it was blood, they ran back and asked if someone would go with them. My mum volunteered to go with them. I ran after her, I clasped her arm in my hands and tried to pull her back, I slipped in the blood and fell. Mum walked away and disappeared into the darkness. I stood up and walked back to my seat slipping in the puddles of blood as I went stumbling forward. I couldn't see where I was going, but found my way eventually. The lights flicked and turned back on. I looked around the train and saw the corpses of the other passengers on the train. I threw myself at the train door trying to open it, finally it opened, so I ran, I ran into a large wooded area and hid behind a tree.

When I turned around, I saw briefly a faded face through the window of the train as it drove out of sight. I sat down freezing cold with the image of the murder in my mind as I wept for my parents.

Now today I tell the tale as I am the only one to survive.

Emily Millier (12)
Fort Hill Community School, Basingstoke

Death Up Close

The sun set over Woodland Prison. The huge grey building cast a cold shadow over the village beneath it. A white van crept up to the gate. The tyres screeched as the van came to a halt. It entered but never left.

The walls of the prison were covered with the stench of torture and death. In the centre of the courtyard, was the van. Officers hauled out a screaming man, Jack Tomb. He bawled as he was dragged through the iron gates, into prison hell. Jack was cast into the cell and locked away.

The sun rose the next morning, as did the rats. They scurried between his legs and finding what crumbs of food they could. Jack was pushed into a cell, with his new cellmate, Tom. 'You can sleep here,' Tom said.

'Well ... OK I guess.'

They both went through their daily activities, and met again at the cell. They both stayed up talking, but Tom fell asleep. Soon after so did Jack. Quiet echoed through the cells until the stroke of midnight.

The tiles on the roof started moving, and were slipped away. A long scaly grey arm came through the ceiling and picked Jack up by the leg. He tried to scream, but noises were muffled under the noise of the creature. The sun rose next morning and Jack had disappeared. A new inmate named Sam replaced him. Tom greeted Sam and said to him,

'You can sleep here from now on.'

'Well ... OK I guess.'

Matt Mitchell (12)
Hall Green Secondary School, Birmingham

Deep In The Forest

When the sun goes down, light turns to dark. He is there. Deep in the forest he is there. Lurking. Watching. Waiting ...

I was trapped. Darkness. Nothing but darkness. It was there waiting for me. The beast stared me in the eye. Gave a fierce screech. Making my ears bleed and eardrums pop. Actually staring at this beast was like staring at an indestructible force.

I ran. And ran. And ran. Not looking back at the immortal. I knew he was there. Every step of the way he was there, travelling twice as fast as me on those gigantic legs. My heart was pounding out of my chest and my legs were like jelly. The forest seemed never-ending. It seemed I was going deeper. And deeper. And deeper into the forest.

At this point, I looked back. His chainsaw-like teeth were expanding out of his jaw. This beast was indestructible. His sharp nails were pointing in my direction. He also had razor-sharp horns. If I stopped I would be a victim of this beast. Just looking at this beast made my face turn white and made me feel like giving up.

I tripped, falling head first. Making my face get cut on the stones. He grappled my neck. Throwing me 20 feet into the air. Kicking me. Punching me. Harming me severely. Then he grabbed my neck hard ...

Amer Mughal (13)
Hall Green Secondary School, Birmingham

Ghost Story

Once there was a boy and a girl who lived with their grandfather. Now their grandfather was an unusual but kind person. The boy's name was Harry and the girl's name was Harriet. They were brother and sister. They both lived in a house beside a spooky old graveyard.

One day Harry got curious and asked Harriet to go with him to the graveyard. Harriet said, 'No, I've got more important things to do.' Harry didn't listen, so he just dragged her outside to the graveyard. Harriet was shaking like she had never shaken before. Harry wasn't afraid at all, he was just excited. He walked on, still dragging Harriet with him. Harry stopped to look at a strange statue placed on top of a crooked grave. Harriet looked at the statue too. She didn't feel scared, but curious. She also read the grave, she gasped and pointed to the person's last name. 'Look Harry, that's our last name too!' she cried.

Harry did look and he was shocked. Suddenly a gust of wind made the trees rustle.

The owls nearby were making sounds too. Harry and Harriet looked up at the sky. It was all purple and black. It was weird because when they went outside it had been bright and sunny. They felt scared, even Harry, so they went back to their house.

They talked to their grandpa about the grave. He said, 'Well kids, I'll tell you who this person was. As you know, this person's name was Edward Martin. He was my father's father. Do you want me to tell you a story?'

'Yes please, tell us,' said Harry and Harriet together.

So their grandpa started his story, 'Okay now, after Edward's 80th birthday party he said he'd take a walk through the forest near him. So he went. My father felt scared because Edward didn't come home for hours. At midnight, there was a wolf howl sound and after it a scream which sounded like Edward. The next day he had disappeared, but a few weeks later a man was digging and found a hand. He phoned the police and they dug too. An hour later they'd found Edward's body lying in the ground. They had a funeral the next day. Just then a stroke of lightning hit the grave and a statue appeared.

'Scary!' said Harriet.

'Spooky!' said Harry.

'I know,' said their grandpa.

'Come on Harriet, let's play!' Harry said.

Harry and Harriet looked at Edward's grave, but then a bolt of lightning hit his grave and the statue again. Both of them disappeared all at once, even Edward's coffin under the ground. Just then Harry and Harriet heard a voice.

Who could it be?

Gillene Inchoco Dadulla (10)
Ligoniel Primary School, Belfast

The Horror Street

Once upon a time there was a woman called Sophie. One night Sophie was in her bed when all at once she heard a bang and a scream. She looked out of the window.

The street was dark and misty. There was a man standing over a dead body. He had a dagger in his hand and pools of blood were everywhere around. Then he looked up at Sophie and laughed.

Sophie pulled down her blinds as fast as she could but … when she turned round he was standing in front of her.

He lifted his dagger and … down she fell.

Twenty years later a woman called Sarah moved into the same house. A neighbour told her the story of Sophie but Sarah didn't believe it.

That night while Sarah took a nice cup of tea in bed, she heard a bang and a scream.

Sarah looked out of her window, she saw the man who had killed Sophie standing over Sophie's dead body. Sarah pulled down her blinds as fast as she could, but the man was standing there with the same dagger. There was another bang and scream, Sarah lay dead.

The people who lived on the street had to change the name of the street.

No one knows the new name of the street … it could be yours! So tonight when you go to bed don't look out of the window!

Ellen Smith (9)
Ligoniel Primary School, Belfast

The Ghost In The Post Factory

There was once a woman called Shannon who worked in a post factory. Everybody who worked there said there was a ghost in the factory and that you'd want to see it!

So one night when Shannon was doing the night shift and all the men went to the pub she was in the smoking room. Shannon saw something but thought it was the men coming back. She turned to look and she saw a ghost.

The next day everyone said, 'You look like you've seen a ghost!'

'Yes I did see a ghost, last night,' said Shannon nearly crying.

'Not to worry,' said the old man.

So now every time Shannon does a night shift. She makes sure another person is with her and Shannon often sees that ghost but she doesn't worry that much!

Megan Breheney (10)
Ligoniel Primary School, Belfast

The School's Ghost

Up on the hill in a very jolly school there was a boy. He'd heard a rumour that he was afraid of heights. One day he proved to everybody that he wasn't. Everybody stared at him while he climbed up on the window sill. He thought and everybody else thought that he would survive. So then he jumped out of the window, head first. This was the day the school's ghost was born.

Twenty years later, the school was re-opened. One unusual boy, Billy, was the only one who knew about what had happened twenty years ago. He knew this because his own father had watched what had happened. He'd told everybody in the whole school.

Every corner of the building was now full of his gossip. I mean every corner, so that even the ghost got to hear about it. The ghost remembered all about it. The only thing he didn't want to hear, was his death.

The ghost raged with anger. He knew exactly who this person was. So he waited in the boys' toilets. The boy was outside playing football. His hands were dirty so he decided to wash them. He walked into the bathroom and there his head was cut off that very day.

The boy's body was buried. However nobody knows about his head. The ghost kept it very well hidden. Everybody these days knows that story. Investigators tried to find his head but they didn't succeed. As for the ghost, he still haunts the hallways of the school.

Chiara Francesca Banas (11)
Ligoniel Primary School, Belfast

The Ghost Of John

Carrick Fergus Castle has a ghost called John Buttoncap. He was a soldier who fell in love with a local girl.

One night he was supposed to be guarding the castle, but instead he went to see his girlfriend. While he was away, the castle was invaded and a lot of people were murdered.

John Buttoncap arrived at his post not knowing what had happened, when his Commander came up to him and he was put in chains and thrown into the dungeons. He was tried for treason and was to have his head cut off.

As he was going to the block, before he had his head cut off, he said he would come back and haunt the castle. They took his head and threw it down the well, inside the castle, his body was buried outside in the grounds and to this day John Buttoncap can be seen at night when the moon is full, trying to get into the castle for his head.

Hannah Bailey (11)
Ligoniel Primary School, Belfast

Ghost Story

'Boom!' Jason shouted.

I did not even turn to face him, I was used to his corny jokes by now. He fell on the bed laughing hysterically. When he noticed that I hadn't even turned to look at him, he came and stood behind me.

'Hey what are you doing?' he asked.

'None of your business.'

'Come on Lena, tell me.'

I ignored him still, but he kept begging.

'You know you want to, come on!'

'Fine!' I finally shouted. 'It's something I found in Egypt last week when we went on our trip. It's some sort of chest. They say it contains all the formulas and plans the Egyptians used to make the pyramids, and lots more! But they also say, if opened in the wrong way, the consequences might be too deadly!' I gave an exaggerated look of fear, but Jason didn't buy it. 'Fatal, extremely excruciating!'

He rolled his eyes.

I gave up.

'Well I was just trying to get it open.'

'Cool. Let me try!' Jason grabbed the chest from my hands.

'No Jason! Don't!'

It was too late, the chest fell to the floor and flew open.

I watched as smoke surrounded Jason, it looked like ghosts were swallowing him up, as a matter of fact, they were!

I tilted my head back and gave a sadistic laugh.

'At last! Free of Jason at last!' I said out loud.

Just then someone tapped my shoulder, I turned, 'Lena, get up, you'll be late for school.'

Debra Osawo (16)
Loreto Convent, Nairobi

The Midnight Drive

Keisha, Carla and I went out for a midnight drive, as we always did. It was pitch-black and there was no sign of any life, just our sports car's booming music and dazzling yellow lights. The atmosphere was perfect.

Suddenly the car stopped! We were out of petrol. 'Great! Just great!' Keisha screamed.

'What are we going to do? We're in the middle of nowhere!' Carla remarked in a quivery voice.

'Just relax everyone,' I said, 'we'll just call for help.' I tried to use my mobile phone but it was dead, so was Keisha's and Carla's. Just then an owl hooted.

'This is freaky,' Keisha said with fear in her voice.

Carla began to sob silently.

'Attention citizens,' the radio reported, 'a psychomaniac has just escaped from the town asylum and is on the run. Be aware, you have been warned!'

Thud! Thud! Thud! the car roof went. We started to scream so loud Adam and Eve could awaken from their graves.

The windows shattered, glass lying everywhere. A policeman appeared and said, 'What's all the noise for girls? The psychomaniac could be anywhere and anyone ...'

Lydia Gachuhi (16)
Loreto Convent, Nairobi

Field Trip To The Film Room

The photo shop was a place we frequented but since we usually stayed at the counter, we knew almost nothing about the dark film room.

This day, we had a chance for exploring the photo shop and the film room. To me it was a fabulous idea but to many of my club mates it was just a field trip. As we entered the room, my excitement got the better of me and I started stretching my hand for the hanging negatives. The instructor had warned us not to but no one bothered to stop me. Looking further into the dark room. I spotted a dark alley. At the end of the alley, there was a small shining spot that seemed to be a keyhole to a brighter room. I crept silently to my new expedition.

Walking down this alley took longer than I thought, the alley seemed longer than it had been earlier. I turned back to see something like a shadow get past me across the alley, but also in time to see it disappear. A door closed in front of me, locking me in. I started to call.

'Help!' my voice echoed bluntly against the walls. 'Help! Anyone, help me!'

I then heard footsteps and stopped calling for help. Curiosity led me to the source of the disturbance. People with long black robes came into view and a person lying on a surgical bed with blood dripping down. These creatures were surrounding the bed and hissing creeds ... suddenly they turned in my direction.

Sarah Itambo (17)
Loreto Convent, Nairobi

That Spider In Her Dream

'Shelly!'

'Jess!' The two friends called out to each other. It all started with one spider and now the whole neighbourhood was chasing after them. They ran as fast as their little legs could take them, but the neighbourhood was behind them, coming slowly like zombies possessed by some demon.

'I can't - I can't breathe,' Shelly was lying down panting for air.

'What! No Shelly, you cannot be having an asthma attack, not now!'

Jess tried to lift her friend but to no avail, Shelly was too heavy for her. She had to think fast because their predators were coming and they got closer by each pant Shelly made.

'Jess, Jess!' Jess turned to find her brother calling her. She ran downstairs, took a glass of water an went to the guest room.

'Whoa! that was one hell of a dream,' Jesse signed in relief.

'Hi Jenny.' Jess' mum was home.

'Ma! It's Jess, the last thing you can do is forget your own daughter's name.'

'Oh sorry, I'm not feeling well, I think I'm coming down with a fever,' she replied heading towards the kitchen.

Jess switched on the television and the news was on.

'A kind of virus is on the outbreak, symptoms are flu and forgetfulness. According to research, they say it could be caused by some kind of spider, stay tuned for more on this story.'

'B-o-r-i-n-g,' Jess shrugged.

Then she remembered what happened earlier.

'The cold! Jenny! Spider! My dream! Oh my God, Mum!'

Jacinta Karanja (16)
Loreto Convent, Nairobi

Ship Of Nightmares

'Don't touch that!' said the ship's treasurer, Jake.

'Why?' I asked. 'What's in it?'

Jake looked at me and gestured me to sit down. He sat down himself.

'Like your tattoo.'

'Legend has it that that chest of gold was from the tomb of the Pharaohs of Egypt. It was cursed. It said, 'Whosoever removes this chest shall receive Hell on Earth'. But the explorers couldn't leave it behind. They didn't believe in the curse. They hauled the chest out of the tomb and the explorers split up the chest's wealth and went their separate ways.

Everything was fine until the full moon appeared and the weirdest feeling went down their spines. The blood ring around the moon confirmed it, the curse was coming true. Food and drink couldn't satisfy them - they felt no warmth or cold, they felt nothing physical, and on the three nights of the full moon, they reflected their true nature. They were living dead. Ghosts. Only the blood of the virgin who bore Pharaoh's mark could set them free. It is said they're still searching for her.'

'That's a good story Jake.'

'Anne, do you believe in ghosts?' he asked as the light from the full moon streamed down on the ship. 'Well I would start if I were you.'

I turned to Jake and his crew only to see them as all ghosts. They drew out their knives as I screamed for mercy!

Natalie Kimani (15)
Loreto Convent, Nairobi

Spook

One sunny afternoon Angel was walking through the forest. After six hours it got very dark. Suddenly Angel heard laughing, just like a witch's laugh. She was very scared. Angel walked five steps forward and saw a house. She walked up to the door and knocked but whoever lived there didn't open the door, so Angel pushed hard on the door and it opened. Angel went inside and heard a big bang! Angel then realised that the door had locked her in.

All of a sudden Angel saw a shadow on the wall. She was terrified and she shouted, 'Help, help!' It looked like a ghost, it was so spooky. She jumped and jumped. She had to get away. Angel tried to jump out of the window to escape but luckily someone saw her and rescued her. She was so grateful she took him out for dinner.

Ria Nathwani (7)
North Primary School, Southall

Don't Look Under Your Bed

It all started when a little boy called Max was playing in his sister's room. He knew his sister, who was called Jessy, would get angry if she saw him playing in her room. Max was only doing it to make her lose her temper.

An hour later, Max fell asleep because his sister didn't turn up. While he was sleeping, his toy truck, which was in his hand, fell on the floor and made a big *thud!* Max woke up and couldn't find his truck anywhere. He looked under the bed and somehow he was sucked into another dimension . . .

'Argh!' Max screamed. *'Uh!* Yuck! I've landed on a, uh ... a ... a maximised sandwich. How can someone eat this peanut butter with tomato and lettuce sandwich?' and he made a funny face.

Then Max saw a fearsome bogeyman carrying a large sack with something big inside it. He was scared because the bogeyman had eyes like a serpent, nails as long as a piece of A3 paper and a nose as long as a 15cm ruler.

Max wanted to find out what was in the big sack. Suddenly he saw the sack move. 'Help! Help! Somebody please help me!' emerged a voice from the sack.

'Jessy, is that you?' cried Max.

'Max ... Max ... is that you? What are you doing here? It's not safe. Anyway, just help me, the bogeyman is a dangerous person. If you see a rope, just tie it around him,' shouted Jessy.

'OK,' shouted Max back. Straightaway Max tried to find a rope; after ten minutes of searching around the bogeyman's hideout he found one. Then he tied the rope around the bogeyman.

'Noooooooooo! You fooooool!' cried the bogeyman.

'Come on Max, let's get a move on, otherwise he will get us and cut us into pieces with his sharp nails.'

'OK.'

They jumped out of the bogeymen's dimension and went flying across Jessy's room. As soon as they landed upside-down they quickly sealed the entrance to the bogeyman's dimension, but the bogeyman stuck his hand out and scratched Jessy on the face. Max reached out for a nail clipper and clipped off all his fingernails because the bogeyman never cut his nails. The bogeyman screamed as loud as he could. *'Argh!* That hurts ... stop it please ... *argh!'* The bogeyman freed himself and stormed into Jessy's room and tried to kill them...

All that time Jessy's and Max's parents were downstairs not knowing what was going on upstairs in Jessy's room. When they heard the noise they rushed into Jessy's room and found the bogeyman seconds away from killing Jessy and Max.

The window in Jessy's room was wide open. The bogeyman looked around and thought he would jump out of the window and escape, but one thing he didn't know was that there was no escape out of that window. That window led him to his death.

'That was close, wasn't it kids? Let's never speak of a bogeyman ever again,' puffed their dad.

Nathan John (10)
North Primary School, Southall

My Ghost Story

Once upon a time there was a mysterious tree. Everybody stayed away from there. But there was one person who parked his car underneath the tree.

One morning he woke up and when he looked at his car he saw the window was broken. He went out to check what damage had been done. The next night he hid near the car to watch and he saw lots of ghosts coming from the tree. They were really funny and were playing a catch game. One ghost saw the man hiding near the car. He picked him up and said, 'How are you old chap?'

'The man was really confused and said, 'How . . . d-d-did my car window get s-s-smashed?' He could hardly speak!

The ghost replied, 'We were playing catch with the ball and it smashed the car window. I'm sorry.'

The next day the man went to the village and told the people what had happened during the night. They wouldn't believe him, they thought he was talking rubbish. However, one man trusted him and together they went and hid under the car when night came. They saw a white trail going round and then whole ghost body came up. *'Argh!'* There's a ghost!'

The village people all came running to the tree and they also saw the ghost. The man told them, 'Don't worry, they are friendly,' and from that day on, everyone became friends with the ghosts.

Kirpal Kaur Deoora (8)
North Primary School, Southall

The Ghost Party

One cloudy, cold night in the haunted house there lived a ghost called Tom. Tom lived on the top of a hill with his friends, Jack and Bob. 'Shall we have a party?' asked Tom to his friends.

'Yes. what a great idea,' said Bob.

'OK then, we'll have a party on Friday, how does that sound?' They all agreed.

The next day, Tom, Jack and Bob were calling all their friends to make sure they would be able to come on Friday. They had just two days to sort out all the party arrangements.

Tom was in a right state, he rushed into his room to find his address book to see if there was anyone he had missed out. All of a sudden, *bang!* He slipped on some marbles he had left out when he had been playing with Jack at the weekend. He had forgotten to put them away. 'Ow, that hurt!' he said. He looked around but there was no one to help him. He stared at his room, *what a mess,* he thought. He cleaned it up.

Next day, which was Thursday, Tom, Jack and Bob started to put up, or shall I say, down, the decorations. All around the house, they were on the banisters, on the floor, everywhere except on the walls or ceiling. What a mess!

They went to bed really tired. On Friday morning they woke to make the food for the party. What they did not realise was that the electricity had gone off during the night and came back on early in the morning. All the clocks were wrong. They thought the time was 11am when it was actually 3.30pm.

The doorbell rang and Bob went running down the stairs to open the door. Halfway down the stairs he slipped on some decorations; behind him were Tom and Jack. *Bang, bang, bang!* All fell on top of each other and were in a lot of pain.

More and more ghosts started to ring the bell but the boys could not get up from the floor because they were in so much pain. Finally Tom managed to get up and open the door and all his friends came in, turned on the music and danced away into the night.

What no one realised was that Tom, Jack and Bob had not got around to making any food. I don't think anyone even noticed!

Nikisha Panesar (9)
North Primary School, Southall

The Haunted Mystery

In a house where the darkness of night hung over trees blowing eerily around, there lived a family of three - Mum, Dad and eleven-year-old Kate. 'Dinner's in the oven, Kate!' shouted Mum. She and Dad were going out for the evening.

Slam! went the door.

Kate was really hungry - she turned on the microwave, which after a few seconds suddenly switched off and all the lights went out 'This is spooky!' said Kate and ran upstairs and lay on her bed for a few minutes, then got up and tried to call someone from her mobile - no credit! The windows flew open and she tasted the damp rain and heard creaks in the darkness - this was the season she truly hated - winter.

Slowly and bravely she stood up and went up into the attic - she got her laptop out and when she logged on there was a message saying 'You'll see my dear, wait till it strikes 9pm!' - Only ten minutes left!

Kate ran back to her bedroom - she was now hysterical - crying loudly and shaking. She heard someone talking to her, 'This is my house, I lived here five years ago; on Hallowe'en night I was murdered, I didn't want to die; like me you will now die...'

Kate screamed and screamed, she felt a tap - it was her mum who hugged her and said, 'Don't worry, darling you're safe now.'

Kate heard the ghost's mocking laughter ... 'You wait ...'

Harpreet Karwal (11)
North Primary School, Southall

Imagination

It happened just this afternoon, I came back from school to have lunch. There I was in the bathroom and the door just went *bang!* The water went *drip-drop! Drip-drop!* I was scared!

When I was walking back to school, it seemed as though someone was following me! I looked back and saw no one. I was even more scared!

In school the afternoon went badly; you see I had detention because I hadn't done my homework.

Finally, it was home time. As I was walking home with my friend, Nikki, I saw a dead pigeon. I felt really bad and frightened but then remembered I'd forgotten my homework and as I didn't want to get detention again, I rushed back, letting Nikki meet me by Tomson's alley.

I ran past Bob's Bakery, into Simon's alley and into the school gate. 'Thank God it wasn't shut …' I went into class and turned the lights on but when I turned my back, the lights went off. I was nervous and my legs were shaking. I quickly got the homework from the table and suddenly ran into someone. When I looked back I saw Henry the caretaker! I was glad it wasn't anyone else.

I got home tired and hungry, so after a snack I went to have a little nap.

Drip-drop! Drip-drop!

Ttt-tttt! My teeth were moving, I was scared! I got up and went to look … I saw Mum fixing the leak.

'I think I'm imagining things,' I said to myself

Sundus Sayeed (11)
North Primary School, Southall

What Was That?

It was a cold, windy night. The angry wind was howling, the trees were dancing in the wind. At the edge of a forest there lived a family, a mum, a dad and two twin sisters. One was named Lucy, she was bossy, and the other named Rosie, who was very kind. Lucy used to tease Rosie about being scared of ghosts. Rosie used to get fed up. She had a plan.

One stormy night Rosie scared Lucy. She got a white sheet and put it around her body. She looked like a real ghost. Lucy ended up screaming. The night remained silent and peaceful until there was a scream, it was coming from their wardrobe which was placed in the corner of their room.

'Rosie, stop it, it's not scary, it's just annoying now,' moaned Lucy.

'But ... that wasn't me ... it's com ... coming from the wardrobe,' mumbled Rose; the screaming continued.

'Argh!' screamed the twins as they ran into their parents' room.

'What happened?' asked their mum. While she was asking, a white ghost entered the room. The twins screamed again. The ghost stood at the door. It was coming closer and closer. It was face to face with the twins.

'Argh!' screamed the twins again.

'Wake up, you just had a nightmare, we'll talk about it in the morning,' Mum sweetly said to them.

As Mum walked out and the door shut, suddenly the wardrobe started to shake. The twins screamed ... !

Jaspreet Kaur Sidhu (11)
North Primary School, Southall

Ghost Dog

Kim, her mum and her dad, lived in a big city. In the garden it was like a little yard where just bins were kept. Her mum and dad were arguing because Kim wanted a pet dog. To cheer her up and make it up to her, they gave Kim stuffed dogs, china dogs and all sorts. They bought her posters of dogs and filled her shelves with books on dogs.

But one day, their lifestyle changed. Dad got a new job. They left their old house and moved into a little house with a big garden. There was also a field beyond the garden and Kim thought it was the perfect place for a dog.

A dog had lived there once and Mum had complained about the smell. She had gone to the supermarket for an air freshener so it wouldn't stink anymore.

As Kim leapt into bed in her empty, new room, she thought she heard a dog barking and howling. It sounded close by. She climbed out of bed to investigate. The branches made weird, squeaky noises with the moaning of the wind.

Kim shivered. She scurried back to bed and pulled the duvet over her head. She thought, *if only there had been a dog in the garden! A big, friendly dog to keep guard.* And there it was! A lovely white dog. But, where did it go? Kim knew she had seen something. Unless it was a ... ghost!

Fariha Sahab (11)
North Primary School, Southall

The Day Evil Struck North Primary

It was Sunday, but all the teachers were stuck in boring school marking the state's exam papers. The teachers had to come in as they were behind schedule, but the pupils were enjoying themselves at home.

It would not be boring for long for the teachers; did I tell you about a man named Can Dracula? This Can character had the ability to shoot beans from his can body in the morning and in the afternoon he could 'wipe out' anything in his way with Coca-Cola. Talk about unhealthy!

The Can man had other villainous mates too, Mad Mud Mike and George the Ghost. Together this evil trio planned to take over the world.

Mike was the maddest mud man in the world; by shooting mud from his body he could turn anything into solid mud. He had the power to shoot from very long distances. Mike was proud to be known as the most disgusting member of the team.

Ghostly George who had won first place in 'Ghost Scarer of the Year 2006' competition looked your average white sheet ghost but don't be fooled, he is your worst nightmare!

Back to the bored teachers, or maybe it's going to get more exciting, for Mr Logan and Miss Kennedy. Mr L and Miss K were in the staffroom when over the PA system they heard their names called out by Mrs Grewal. Mrs G's garbled message was *'Ehberfvbv! Egwe'* - Mr Logan and Miss Kennedy!

The dastardly trio had struck. They had intercepted Mrs Grewal's emergency message with their laser -gobble-de-whoo-who gun. Mr L and Miss K fell straight into the trap by running towards Mrs G's office. Waiting for them on the way to the office were the bad guys.

But sometimes, the bad guys were just too stupid.

By mistake, George scared his nasty accomplice with his evil screech. *'Whoooo! Whoooo! Bhoooo! Bhoooo!'*

Mad Mud Mike jumped at the screeching and shot mud at George, which turned him solid instantly. Can Dracula panicked and shot beans and Coke all over Mad Mud Mike, knocking Mike out. Dracula made a run for it but fell over his muddy mate and was stuck in the mud. Dracula shouted out, 'Mummy, help me!'

Everybody thought Mr L and Miss K were heroes. The teachers handcuffed the baddies and the school was safe once more.

Harkirat Kler (8)
North Primary School, Southall

The Ghost Boy

Tom's father was a ghost hunter. The ghosts his father hunted, loved eating *babies!*

Tom also had a baby sister called Sally. She was the prettiest little baby ever to be born in the little town of Greenwood. All of Tom's friends and family came to see little Sally. 'Tom, aren't you so lucky to have a little sister,' they all said.

Tom was jealous of Sally so he thought to himself that if he started to act like a baby he, too, would get all the attention from everyone, especially his mum and dad. So in the middle of the night he got up and started to cry like a baby. Mum and Dad jumped out of bed and ran into Tom's room. *'I want my bottle!'* moaned Tom.

'If you don't stop this right away the ghosts will come and get you. They don't like big cry babies.'

Tom didn't listen, he carried on crying, Mum and Dad ignored him and walked away. 'We warned you, Tom.'

Suddenly Tom heard howling and he went quiet. The wolves had heard Tom crying like a baby. That very next moment, Tom started to shrink, he couldn't understand what was happening and, before he knew it, all that could be heard was the sound of a baby crying from his room.

'It's happened,' said Dad to Mum.

'Well, we did warn him, my dear,' replied Mum.

The ghosts took Tom away and he was never seen again.

Simrath Sehmi (9)
North Primary School, Southall

The Green Ghost

Hannah, ten years old, has pretty blue eyes, is 4.5 feet tall and has an annoying little brother. Mike, five years old, has green eyes, loves reading frightening comic books and hates Hannah.

Suddenly Hannah woke and she heard a noise. It sounded like a knock on her bedroom wall, then an idea came into her head, it was probably her brother but she couldn't remember, she was so sleepy. Then she got up to check if it was her brother. 'What is it now?' questioned Hannah sleepily.

'I'm scared of the Green Ghost - I heard a noise from my cupboard,' whispered Mike.

'Oh Mike, I told you that ghosts are not real!' shouted Hannah angrily.

'Sorry, but I just can't get it out of my mind,' replied Mike tearfully.

'Why don't you read a book? That's what helps me go to sleep, go on!' exclaimed Hannah grumpily. She then went back to her bedroom. There she started shouting, *'Help! Help!'* but there was no reply, Mike didn't come out of his room either.

The ghost who was named the Green Ghost was really alive; she had just seen a picture of him in Mike's book. She ran into Mike's room and they both dashed downstairs but Dad was not there and Mum had gone to work. So they ran into the basement and locked the door.

Something, someone ... was in the basement, but what was it? What was it doing in there? How did it get there ... ? It was a mouse. Hannah began to rip the pages of the book and then she found a picture of the ghost and she ripped it.

'Wake up Hannah, wake up!' shouted Mike unhappily.

'Are you OK? Did you get hurt?' exclaimed Hannah, frightened.

'Yes, of course I'm OK, why are you being so nice to me all of a sudden?' screamed Mike, confused.

But Hannah did not reply.

Disha Ghelani (9)
North Primary School, Southall

The Ghost Trick

One happy night on Hallowe'en, Roxy decided to see her next-door neighbour, Sasha. She had long red hair and was 13 years old. Sasha was her friend. She didn't know much about Sasha; they'd just met in high school.

She was about to knock next door when she saw a sign, Sasha had moved out! 'I wonder who lives here now?' Roxy asked herself, feeling confused.

She crept up to the door and sneaked in. She saw fake cobwebs around her as if nobody had lived there for ages. She could hear her own heart beating fast. She smelt trouble. She felt she should leave.

Suddenly the door closed behind her, it was locked! She didn't know what to do. 'Oh no, it won't open, I can't get out!' Roxy screamed nervously. She heard footsteps coming towards her but she saw nothing.

She tried to pinch herself to wake up as she thought it was just a dream. Trying hard to be brave, she called for help. Nobody came. She went in a weird room and saw ghosts everywhere! She was frightened and ran to the door. The ghosts followed her!

She forgot the door was locked. The ghosts unlocked the door with their special oil. Roxy opened the door and saw the owners of the house standing in front of her. They looked scary, old and tired. Finally Sasha took off her mask, it was a trick!

'Got you!' Sasha cried.

'Whoa, you scared me!' Roxy replied.

'Well, it is Hallowe'en,' Sasha remarked.

Did Roxy know that? What should she have done? Who would she tell? She needed to trick her back.

She became happy. She began to sleep peacefully. She thought about the trick for Sasha. Immediately she began to laugh and laugh. She saw that she was lying in the bed. It was just a dream! Roxy was upset. She loved her dream. She wished it was never over.

Samera Iqbal (9)
North Primary School, Southall

The Wall Of Faces

'Maria Goniez - died tragically aged 17 ...'

Etched on a deserted gravestone in a lone graveyard, our news team was convinced that her tombstone hid a deeper, eerie secret. The village locals couldn't remember what had happened to her all those years ago but someone did. The mad, old woman who lived on top of the hill!

My news partner and I made our way up to see her. It was a warm, late afternoon but there was a chill in the air as we reached her eerie cottage. We knocked and waited with a mixture of excitement and dread! Our search for the unsolved mystery had finally brought us to this door ...

The door creaked open and, upon letting us in, slammed shut behind us! We could make out a wall and a figure, with long hair which was white, greeted us, 'Who comes for Maria's story?'

I answered slowly, 'I do.'

She called me closer and as I approached, she suddenly grabbed my hand and leaned into the light - a scary, gnarled, old, toothless woman! She told us that Maria could see spirits from the other side and wanted to learn from the woman how to pass over to see her dead mother. The old woman promised her she could - in return for a gift.

As she held my hand, the wall behind her began to change into hundreds of screaming faces, one of which was my newspaper partner's! I turned around to find him but he'd disappeared!

I pulled away from the clutches of the old woman as she cackled, 'Thank you for my precious gift, my child. Your friend will miss you but I need you to go tell the world Maria's story! *Ha! Ha! Ha! Ha! ...*'

The question was, however, who would believe me now?

Suhavi Narula (10)
North Primary School, Southall

The Bloodsucking Ghost

One dark, rainy day, people on the street were wearing thick waterproof jackets. Cars had their windscreen wipers on. Not a single umbrella was closed - red and yellow tops were everywhere. When the rain finally stopped, hardly anyone was left on the streets, but it was still dark.

There was a man with a hood on; his face couldn't be seen! He walked slowly and suspiciously into a gloomy alley. *'Aarrgghh!'* was the sound that wailed out.

The next day, the news presenter reported that a man had been found dead but only his face was found. Most people stayed at home. Some went out, but not into the alleys. Some did go into the alleys, but then mysteriously disappeared.

One family became very anxious - two children (Luke and Ben) and their parents.

'If we don't get rid of this ghost and its soul that haunts the alley, then this thing is going to kill off almost everyone!' wailed Luke.

'Yeah! We will warn everyone not to go into a certain alley otherwise ... you know what will happen ...' whispered Ben.

So, Ben and Luke told the whole world (even the news reporters) that there was a ghost in one alley. *'Do not go there!'* announced Luke.

'We did it. We did it,' cheered the boys.

Do you know what happened to the ghost? Well ... let's just say he is still alive. Mostly every night there is a loud scream, *'Help me!'*

Hanish Panesar (10)
North Primary School, Southall

The Melted Ghost

It was 12 midnight and Gabrielle was leaving with her family to move into a house in town. The house they were moving to was 100 years old and nobody had lived there for years. Gabrielle was scared!

When they got to the house Gabrielle had to go to bed because it was almost 2am. She was walking upstairs when she heard something go *'Boo hoo!'* Gabrielle started shivering with fear! She walked into her bedroom and saw something floating in the air, it looked like a ghost! Gabrielle was so petrified she couldn't even scream for help.

She ran downstairs and got a bucket of water and ran all the way back upstairs to her room. She threw the water on the figure in the air and the figure melted.

Gabrielle thought to herself, *can the house be haunted*? Gabrielle sat and thought and thought until one day she found out in the newspapers that it was. From that day Gabrielle watched her steps wherever she went and the mystery of the haunted house could not be solved.

Camielle Tamara Mattan (8)
North Primary School, Southall

The Ghost Story

One day a boy called Mac went to a haunted hotel with his dad, Max. As they reached the hotel, Mac asked his dad, 'Don't you think this hotel is a little bit scary?'

'No, it is not scary,' replied his dad. 'Come with me.'

Both Mac and Max went in and saw six doorways. Mac wanted to go through the second door, while his dad wanted to go through the sixth door. However, before both of them could decide which door to go through, five ghosts jumped from above them and started coming towards them. The ghosts got closer and closer to Mac and Max and suddenly they jumped on them laughing loudly and shouting, 'We are going to turn you into ghosts like us. Run if you can, but if we catch you, you will not escape from our power and us,' said the ghosts together.

Max suddenly thought of an idea, to get a rope and put it round the ghosts' bellies and spin them round and round. They got a rope out of their bag and tried to catch the ghosts with it. The ghosts dodged the rope and flew away.

Out of nowhere a magic lamp appeared near where Mac and Max were standing. The lamp was made of shiny copper and when they rubbed it, one by one, the ghosts disappeared into the lamp.

Suddenly there was a loud clapping sound. When they looked to see where the sound had come from, Mac and his dad saw the owner of the haunted house. He informed Mac and Max that the ghosts had been in his house for the last ten years and had made his life a misery.

At long last the man could live happily ever after in his house with his wife and two small children. He thanked both Mac and Max.

Gurjit Virdee (8)
North Primary School, Southall

A Spooky Night

Rob and his twin brother, Bob, went to play in the park just after they had finished their tea. It was a reasonably good afternoon and they played until sunset. On the way from the park to their house, a graveyard had to be passed.

Rob said, 'Let's go through the graveyard, it will be much faster.'

'I'll give you a race,' said Bob.

As the children were running through the park they suddenly heard a noise. They were scared as the noise was getting closer. Rob saw a big figure flying in the air. He didn't know what it was. Bob and Rob ran back home.

When they got home they both ate their supper. Mum thought the boys were very quiet and she asked them if everything was alright. They said they were fine and went to bed. They decided never to go to the spooky graveyard again.

Sikander Bhinder (8)
North Primary School, Southall

The Night I Dreamt Of A Ghost

Last night I had a dream about a ghost.

My mummy put me to bed at 8 o'clock. She gave me a kiss and a cuddle and said, 'Goodnight, sweet dreams.' I closed my eyes and went to sleep.

I started dreaming. In my dream I saw a ghost. He was a funny ghost and not scary at all. I am usually scared of ghosts, but I wasn't scared of this ghost because he was friendly. He reminded me of a clown. He was very colourful and he had a big smile. I knew he was a ghost and not a clown because he said to me, 'Hello Simran, my name is Chintu and I am a ghost, but I am not a horrible ghost, I am a friendly ghost who likes children.'

He asked me if I would like to go to the funfair and I said, 'Yes.'

We went on the roller coaster and on the Twister, my favourite rides. We also went on the bumper cars. We had popcorn and candyfloss to eat and also some hot dogs. We had lots of fun.

It started to get dark and Chintu said to me, 'Simran, we need to go home now.'

I said, 'Okay, thank you for taking me to the funfair.'

Suddenly my mummy was waking me up to go to school. She said, 'Did you sleep well Simran?'

I said, 'Oh yes, Mummy,' and I had a big smile on my face, just like Chintu's smile.

Simran Ram (8)
North Primary School, Southall

Charlie And His Very Helpful Ghost

Charlie was a very lucky boy and he had a ghost in his house. The ghost went downstairs and opened the door. In the living room the ghost put the TV on. Mum went into the room and said, 'Oh good, my favourite programme is on.'

The ghost turned the TV off. Mum was not happy. She said, 'Who did that?' She tried to turn the TV on but each time, a hand grabbed her arm, but there was no one there!

Someone knocked on the door. It was the TV man. He said, 'If you turn your TV on, it will explode.'

Charlie knew he was a lucky boy because the ghost had saved his mum, so Charlie called the ghost 'Lucky'!

Charlie Kirk (8)
North Primary School, Southall

Help!

One day I was sitting on the sofa and I was watching a football match on TV while my baby sister was sleeping. I looked at her and thought to myself, *she won't wake up for another hour,* so I went upstairs. When I reached my room I switched on my computer and started to play some computer games. After about half an hour I looked at my watch and saw that it was already 6 o'clock.

All of a sudden, I heard a big bang! I ran downstairs to see if my baby sister was all right. I looked around the house to see if she was hiding. When I looked at the wall there was something written on it, it said, 'I'm coming to get you!' When I went to get help I saw slime marks on the floor so I followed them into a dark pathway. That's when I saw my baby sister on the floor crying her eyes out and she looked as if she had just seen the ghost.

I tried to help her but I was too scared to go. I shouted, 'Help Mum! Dad, come here!' When they saw me they ran towards me. I told them the problem. As soon as they saw my sister they ran towards her to see if she was all right. While they were there a scary ghost appeared and got them. I ran and called the police.

By the following day the ghost was caught in a vacuum, never to be seen again!

Mitul Nirmal (8)
North Primary School, Southall

The Haunted House

It was a cold, moonless night; the whole family had come home from the shops. I looked at the haunted house next door, it had not been lived in for over a year since the family who lived there had been haunted by ghosts. The windows were sealed, only the doors remained unsealed.

I was carrying a bag of candles and matches. I stepped into the house and I looked around, there were no windows to give any light.

Suddenly a huge, spooky, ghostly figure of my great grandfather appeared before me and warned me I was in great danger from other ghosts. I asked him, 'How do I escape?' He told me that ghosts were afraid of fire then he disappeared.

I quickly ran to the room where the ghosts were all huddled up and stopped at the door. I remembered I had candles and matches in my bag. I knew I was not allowed to play with fire but it was the only way I could stay alive. I lit a candle and threw it at the ghosts. Suddenly the whole house was on fire, I was doomed!

Eeek! went the car brakes.

'Argh!' I yelled.

'What's up?' asked Mum.

'Nothing,' I replied.

I went back into my house and I looked at the haunted house next door. From then on I thought, *there is no such things as ghosts. There's a mystery to that house which will never be solved!*

Simranjeet Duhra (7)
North Primary School, Southall

The Light Saved Me!

It was very cold. Downstairs the clock struck midnight. The house was quiet apart from the creaking floor.

The wind was howling outside and I woke up. I got out of bed and tiptoed downstairs. As I opened the kitchen door I heard a strange noise. It came from the cupboard in front of me. I slowly walked towards it with both my hands in front of me. I reached to open the door but it opened by itself!

I jumped back, shivering with fear. Sitting in the cupboard trying to reach into the bin was a strange white figure. He looked at me and smiled. I then realised I could see through him, but that meant he was a ghost! I walked back a step and then another. I ran to the cupboard and shut it.

Suddenly the ghost flew out of it. He sat on the ceiling light and looked at me, then jumped off the light screaming because the light was hitting him. I didn't know what it meant!

I ran upstairs as fast as I could but the ghost was too fast. He went through me and trapped me. 'Now you can't get out.'

Suddenly I knew I could walk into him and get out so I did. I ran to my room. As I passed the ghost I turned on the light and the ghost entered the room. He seemed to get smaller as I watched him, then I realised that with light he would melt. I ran to my bed and got my torch and shone it at him. He screamed and disappeared.

My mum ran into the room at the sound of the scream. She asked if I was OK. I smiled. It was the first of many adventures.

Arvind Sidhu (8)
North Primary School, Southall

Gabby And The Ghost

One day Gabby went to the fair with her dad and brother. Her brother's name was John. John was in charge of the money for the family, so he bought tickets and took Gabby and Dad to the haunted house. Gabby turned around to hold Dad's arm, but Dad had disappeared. Gabby started to cry but it was too late. Gabby was in front of the *ghost!* The ghost shouted, 'Gabby McNiffin!' She was terrified. She did not know what to do ... so she screamed and the ghost jumped. Gabby ran but as Dad had quickly got changed, he ran after her; soon he caught up with her. John followed soon after.

Gabby said, 'I saw a real ghost.'

John teased her: *'Ah hah hah hah hah!* You are a scaredy-cat!'

Dad politely said, 'Don't be frightened, didn't you recognise your pot-bellied father?'

'Oh! It was you ... Dad!' exclaimed Gabby. 'Now can we have a go on *my* rides?'

They all had a nice time on the teacups, the train and most of all, the ponies. However, John said, 'It is just not fair, Gabby gets to do whatever she wants, and I don't. It's not fair.'

'What do you mean ...? This is the fair!' replied Dad.

Anyway John checked his pocket for money but there was none there - someone had taken it all! Then he turned around and saw a real ghost! *'Argh!'* shouted John.

Joanna Chandra (8)
North Primary School, Southall

Scary Time

It was a dark, stormy day and I had just arrived at the new house. The wind was blowing and there was thunder and lightning. I was very annoyed about the wind because I could not stand still. After a while it started to rain.

As soon as I went into the house I ran upstairs into my room to get changed but I found out that red paint was leaking all over the room. I did not recognise what it was! As I stepped closer to the red paint, I could smell blood. I could also see a lot of writing all over the wall. I started to read all the writing. I wondered who had written all of this. As I was walking towards the bathroom, I saw a trail of blood on the floor. I was so frightened I started to shiver!

I started screaming for help! After a few minutes, my mum came to help me. When my mum came upstairs, she asked, 'Why were you screaming?'

I replied to Mum, 'I saw a huge dead body in the bathroom!'

My mum phoned the police and she let the police know what had happened in the house; she told the police to come and check for any evidence that might be in the house.

Karsana Muhunthan (8)
North Primary School, Southall

Frightening Ghost

It was a dark and scary night. Sam went to bed and soon he was snoring loudly. His mum and dad went to bed at the same time as Sam. It was a snowy night and it was windy.

The snow and wind stopped. Sam woke up. He saw a ghost with a white blanket covering him. Sam couldn't scream, his voice was too sore. Sam whispered to himself, 'I wish I could scream.' Sam tried to do something but he had no ideas.

The door opened by itself and made a sound and then the ghost appeared and came closer and closer to Sam. Sam was frightened, he was shaking and couldn't stop.

Sam turned around as he did not want to see the ugly ghost. When he turned back again the ghost wasn't there anymore! Sam was glad that the ghost had disappeared. The ghost had come in because the window had been open wide.

The next morning Sam went downstairs and told his mum and dad but they didn't believe him. Sam then went to school and told his friends and they were shocked!

Harsimrat Heer (8)
North Primary School, Southall

The Mysterious Family

Tony and Fred had been best friends since the beginning of Year 4. However, Tony had never met Fred's parents. The only time he saw his mum and dad was when they came to school to collect him because they had to go to a funeral. When Tom once asked Fred if he would come over to stay at the weekend, Fred replied, 'Sorry, Tony, but we are going to the seaside; it's my mother's birthday.' However, that weekend, Tony saw Fred playing in the garden. At school, Fred told him, 'We had a fantastic time at the seaside.'

'That was nice,' replied Tony and carried on with his classwork. He did not speak to Fred for the whole week.

One day, Tony was playing in the park near Fred's house, when the ball bounced into Fred's house through the door that was open. Tony walked in, 'Fred,' he shouted. No reply. 'Is anyone home? It's Tony, can I come in to get my ball please?'

There was no answer so he tiptoed further inside to get his ball. He could see that it was dark inside and smelt of fire. When the front door shut, he saw Fred and his family. 'Tony, my friend, I am sorry for lying to you, but there is something I have to tell you. We are all ghosts! We died in a fire in this house two years ago.'

Tony screamed and ran outside. He never saw Fred at school again.

Ruby Khan (8)
North Primary School, Southall

The Place Of Spooks

One rainy, dull day, a girl called Lucy decided to go to a place named Strange Spooks with her friend Katie. They travelled by coach; it was a thirty minute journey.

Eventually they arrived at the place which looked very terrifying but then Katie and Lucy stepped inside. Katie decided to go into the cloakroom to put their coats away so they did; Lucy opened the door - it made a squeaky sound; they put their coats away and quickly ran out, then Katie panicked, 'It's really creepy in this place.'

'Don't worry, I'm with you,' Lucy assured her.

Just then they both heard footsteps, smelt trouble, felt frightened and saw a blood-splattered alien! They were terrified; they both tried to run as fast as they could, then Lucy questioned, 'Where did this horrible alien come from?'

'I don't know but I'm so scared,' answered Katie.

Suddenly ... the alien grabbed Katie and threw her out of the window, which was very painful. Lucy quickly ran down the stairs but the alien ran faster and grabbed her. Lucy said, 'Let go of me now!' Then the alien accidentally let go of Lucy.

The alien loved to eat humans, so he grabbed Lucy, opened his mouth and ... Lucy shouted, *'Argh!* Where am I?'

'What happened Lucy?' asked Mum.

'Oh ...I just had a bad dream,' she replied.

'Now go back to bed,' Mum said.

All along it had just been a frightening dream!

Sulu Haneefa (9)
North Primary School, Southall

The Ghost Story

One night, Jack, Lucy and Sam went to the Hallowe'en carnival. They were always so scared about the 'House of Horror' rides. Jack went on the ride first because he was the bravest. When he got on he was so petrified!

All of them eventually went on the ride but they were terrified of the ghosts. Suddenly the ride stopped! Immediately it felt like their hearts would pop out of their chests. The rides were powered by electricity which had failed. All around was tense. Everyone was so worried. Their legs went like jelly. They were stuck! What could they do?

The whole world heard that they were stuck on the ride. Relatives, friends and family phoned in asking, 'Where's Jack? Where's Lucy? Where's Sam?' Their parents were extremely worried.

Ten days later, the were free and what a relief it was! When they got home, they were so happy that they watched a horror film that night. They were shivering so much from fright that they got their teddy bears out then went to bed.

That night Jack, Lucy and Sam had sweets, chocolates and loads of junk food. Their mum heard them and she said, 'Jack, Lucy, Sam, what are you doing?'

When they had settled down to sleep, they heard spooky noises. Lucy was shivering with fear. She said, 'Jack, no! Please don't go! Sam, don't go, I will go instead.' Lucy went to check what the noise was. When she came back she said, 'It was just the wind.'

'Thank goodness,' replied Sam and Jack.

Jaskaran Kalsi (9)
North Primary School, Southall

The Invisible Ghost

One cold, frosty afternoon, Oliver was happily walking through a tremendous jungle. He stopped and looked around. Everything was quiet. He walked even further until he saw a house. He started to *shiver!* Oliver decided to go inside even though he was frightened. As soon as he got inside, the door slammed closed. He was very, very scared.

Then suddenly Oliver heard and saw a ghost on the broken terrible ceiling. He was very confused. While Oliver was walking, the ghost kept on moving and following him. Even if he hid, the ghost would be behind him.

There was no way Oliver could get out. Then suddenly he came up with an idea and so he managed to get out of the house and the ghost was never seen again.

Dylan Nathwani (9)
North Primary School, Southall

Vampires

The night before Hallowe'en, Harry got his costume for 'trick or treating'.
'Now I hope you will be careful but have fun,' Mum warned.

The next morning Harry went to school early because of the school play. He was a garlic man. After the play it was break and then a very mysterious thing happened …
Mike, Harry's friend, had tooth-shaped marks on his neck. Harry thought, *I'll leave him alone.* At night Mike took ten minutes for every house he went to. Harry followed him into one house. 'Oh my God,' Harry shouted, 'Mike, you're a vampire, *argh!'*
Mike then followed Harry right out of the door with a gang. Harry ran to the coffee shop and hid near the shopkeeper. 'Do you want a burger?' the shopkeeper asked Harry.
'That's it, garlic kills vampires,' snapped Harry and snatched the garlic burger and ate it.
The gang came in. 'Now vampires will rule the world,' Mike laughed. Harry went up close to them and his breath which smelt of garlic killed all the vampires.

Karanvir Kalsi (9)
North Primary School, Southall

The Spirit Of Bloody Mary

Once there was a boy called John who was a scaredy-cat. John was the youngest and smallest one in his family - a shrimp compared to his two brothers. He lived with his mum and dad.

One rainy day, he remembered what his friends had told him about the spirit of Bloody Mary. Ever since, he had been scared of mirrors because he kept on seeing her face in them and was terrified.

His brothers were playing a game in which they dared each other to do things. John enjoyed this game and he also played. He was hoping that his brothers would not dare him to say 'Bloody Mary' nineteen times.

Soon it was his turn, they dared him to say the deadly phrase nineteen times into the mirror. He stood in one place ... scared. He had no choice.

He went to a mirror and switched off the lights - it was pitch-black. He started saying it slowly up to the third time - the whole room turned red ... faster now to the nineteenth time.

She came and *scratched* his face! He had blood all over his hands and face and a mark of the letter 'M' on his T-shirt.

He quickly found a book and threw it at the mirror. Everything returned to normal but what he didn't know was that he had just received seven years of bad luck! Soon after that, he fainted and fell to the ground.

His mum and dad returned from their dinner; everyone was in shock ...

Navjit Gill (10)
North Primary School, Southall

The Invisible Hand

Mom wanted to buy some books so we went to the shop. When we got there I spotted the perfect one. 'Mom, I want this one,' I said. 'It's called 'The Invisible Hand'.'

'I've chosen my book so let's go home now,' Mom said.

'But I want to get more books.'

'I haven't enough money, I promised Katie I would get her some sweets,' Mom said.

We paid for the books and sweets and went home.

When we got home I jumped into my bed and started reading. I became tired so I put the book under my pillow and tried to sleep but I just couldn't.

Later that night a hand suddenly appeared from the book!

'Oh no, it was exactly what was said in the book. It said: 'When you put the book down you must sleep after two minutes. If you don't, a hand will appear and you will die'.' The hand wrapped itself around my neck and I could not breathe anymore.

In the morning Katie came to my bedroom and saw me lying in my bed. I was dead! Katie went to tell Mom the news. Mom started crying. She went to the shop and slapped the shopkeeper.

From that day on, no one bought any books from the shop ever again.

Aysha Khalid (9)
North Primary School, Southall

The Haunted Castle

Tom and Sophie walked up the spooky hill! When they finally got to the top it was midnight. They saw weird things; they saw a graveyard, some kind of flower that eats everything and, last but not least, they saw a haunted castle!

Both Tom and Sophie were trembling with fear! Tom knocked on the big, high, tall doors. Nobody answered; then he knocked again and, by magic, the doors just opened! Tom and Sophie walked in. *Bang!* The doors slammed!

It was complete darkness inside but then Sophie recognised a light coming from upstairs. They walked up the big, spooky stairs and suddenly, a werewolf appeared! It chased them around the castle.

Suddenly Tom and Sophie disappeared; they were never seen again!

Martin Ghrabie (10)
North Primary School, Southall

What Happened To The People?

'Right,' shouted their father, 'we're moving house. I can't stand the dog barking because it needs some space.'

'I agree,' said Mum.

Kevin and Jack looked excited and the fat dog, Fang, barked.

'Are we moving to 160 Argyle Avenue? It's thought to be creepy,' sneered Jack.

Dad got a phone call, he whispered not to make the twins too excited, 'We're moving to 160 Argyle Avenue.'

'Yes!' screamed Kevin bouncing on the sofa. 'Wait till the children in school hear about this.'

The 10-year-olds packed their bags and belongings and got in the car. They grabbed the keys off their mum and tried to open the door, but surprisingly the door was already open. The children unpacked their bags in their two giant separate rooms. Even Fang got his own room.

That night Fang's room suddenly opened by itself. He wandered off into the massive nine-roomed mansion. Fang was getting tired and felt ill. He collapsed next to the dustbin.

The next morning Kevin found Fang next to the green dustbin, he wasn't moving at all. After a few hours they found out he was dead. They called the detectives and they looked for clues. At night they waited to see what happened. A green light came and everyone died. After a few days maggots had eaten them up. Then they disappeared...

Rehan Rizwan (10)
North Primary School, Southall

The Magic Of Ghosts

Five friends, fed up of cooking every day, appointed a cook: tall, looked grumpy and breathed in an unhealthy manner. He didn't like obeying rules - he only did his job because he loved healthy food. However, he was kind, generous and he had no criminal records. The cook prepared delicious food on a daily basis.

He moved in with the friends. They provided him a room in their mansion. The biggest place was the kitchen - scary and creepy. It was thirty feet long; it would take a month to clean it all. At night, it was a fearful place: banging doors could be heard, creepy ghosts could be felt! Nevertheless, everyone lived happily for a period of time. The cook was slow and was sometimes told off because of his slow speed of work.

One day, unexpectedly, the cook started to work unbelievably fast. The five friends wondered what could be wrong. They started to keep an eye on the cook.

It was a strange evening sunset. The friends sat at the dinner table. John asked for water. The cook obeyed the order. He went to the kitchen corridor. He stood there. John watched him stretch his arms, *twenty feet long,* and take the water from the end of the colossal kitchen. He couldn't believe his eyes. He nearly died of fear. He tried to tell the others but they refused to believe him.

'Ghosts are as white as bread or invisible ...'

'Can he be a ghost?' cried John ...

Shagar Ghelani (10)
North Primary School, Southall

Mudhouse Mansion

Outside Lancaster on Lake Road sits a house, a big house, a house big enough for a family of ten. This house is no ordinary house which is why it is called … Mudhouse Mansion.

There once was a girl called Katie who lived on Lake Road. Every morning and every night Katie found the neighbourhood very strange. One night she heard slight screams and shouting from Mudhouse Mansion so Katie went out into the neighbourhood and went near the house. She saw a sign saying *No Trespassing* but Katie ignored that and she entered the house.

As Katie was going up each floor she heard footsteps in front of her. As Katie reached the top floor, she heard a loud scream coming from a room opposite her and there stood Bloody Mary staring at Katie with pure black eyes. Katie ran down all the stairs, went out the exit and climbed over the driveway gate. She pulled out her camera and took a photo of five ghosts staring out of the broken upstairs windows.

When everyone on Lake Road heard about this they were horrified and decided to do something about it. But right now on Lake Road this house is still there … haunted!

Adanna Bailey (10)
North Primary School, Southall

The Petrifying Day

'Argh!' yelled Simon fearfully as someone or something pranced out of the prickly hedges. He peered inquisitively in all directions immediately but there wasn't anything there ...

That night, when Simon went to bed he thought continuously about the peculiar event that had taken place in his garden. Soon he dozed off but a few hours later he was awoken by a deafening howl coming from the garden.

Simon was really surprised about the fact that his parents were still asleep and he crept silently into the backyard. Curious of the noise, he looked everywhere but once more he couldn't see anything.

The relieved boy was just about to enter the house, when something tugged his gown vigorously. As he swirled around, his eyes filled with horror, while he experienced the sighting of a terrifying ghost. The ghost dragged Simon and vanished through a crevasse and they were never seen again.

Gerrard Jayaratnam (11)
North Primary School, Southall

On Hallowe'en Day

Once upon a time there were two children, Jane and Phil. They were a family and one day they were getting really excited about Hallowe'en which would be the next day. They were deciding what to wear and which costume they wanted.

During the night, they couldn't wait till it was the morning and they were thinking what they were going to do ... At last, it was the morning and also it was Hallowe'en. After they had got dressed and everything, they wanted to visit the haunted castle. So when they reached there, they decided to just look around.

Suddenly, they saw a real ghost and got really, utterly freaked out. They were sweating from head to toe and were just standing there like statues. The ghost was really frightening but it didn't harm them. Unusually, the ghost flew away somewhere so Jane and Phil had enough thinking time to make a really good plan to get out, but it wasn't so easy because all the doors were locked.

Luckily, Jane had a plan and decided to quickly jump out of the window as it was open. So they hurried, one at a time they jumped and they were on the ground. They were safe and were shivering cold. They rushed back home before anything could get worse.

When they arrived home they told everyone but no one could believe them so they just wrote it in their precious diary that they only kept with them.

Sabina Haneefa (11)
North Primary School, Southall

The School Of Horror

Once there was a young girl called Kate. She was five years old. Her dad died whilst fighting a war, Kate and her mother were terribly sad.

Five years later, she was ten years old. She was incredibly smart. She could be described as extraordinary! She was very brave - her kindness was always walking alongside her. She had brown hair and brown eyes: I'm telling you she was quite tall!

One day she had the most weird feeling. She had a flashback, - it was of her dad dying and oh, that must be extremely uncomfortable!

On Wednesday, Kate had a club; the club teacher was missing. 'Oh no! Where could she be?' She wandered around the school. Suddenly, she saw her dad's spirit (she must have been as scared as a mouse, actually now that I've thought about it, she must have been a scared mouse!) The ghost was following her even if she went to the bathroom. Then she heard footsteps. The floorboards were creaking. You can't even imagine how petrified she was. Then she hid in the library. The person up there turned out to be a man.

The man went near the door. He stamped his feet, so it sounded like he was walking away. He then tiptoed back. Kate came out. The man covered her mouth - so she couldn't scream - and threw her in a hole (which he'd made in the basement, which wasn't used). Then he ran away. The spirit followed her, the thing is, only she could see it ...

The hole was dark and spooky. She saw a radio. It made a static noise. 'Hooray, I can get help!' She spotted a phone, as quick as a flash she phoned the radio company. The radio company rescued her. The police put the kidnapper in jail. The club teacher was found tied to a chair.

Ten years later, Kate grew up to be a police officer (and oh, that must be cool!) so that she could rescue the very people who, like her, are thrown in holes sometimes, maybe ...

Amandeep Khera (10)
North Primary School, Southall

The Haunted House

Once upon a time there was a family, in the family there was Sarah, Joe, Steven and Joanna. They lived in a huge mansion but one day Joe said, 'Let's move house,' so they agreed.

They started to pack up their stuff in suitcases and they put everything in the car and drove to their new house. They went inside and ...

The house was all dirty, with dust and spiders' webs everywhere. Then they all cleaned it like a team. As soon as Sarah came down, the room was in a mess again. She left it and went to make tea. Then she went back. When she came down again the tea was already in the cups on the table!

She was so scared she screamed and called Joe. Joe was scared and was shivering. Then they found out that it was spirits of old people who used to live there before. As soon as possible they packed their bags and left.

They went back to their other house and lived happily ever after.

Afia Kamran (10)
North Primary School, Southall

Poor Daisy And Her Walking Wardrobe

Daisy is a ten-year-old girl who is not afraid of anything. She was moving house with her family and when she got to the house she was very excited. Daisy ran upstairs, chose her room before her mum and dad closed the door and put her bags down. When she decided what colour she started to paint it pink. Her mum and dad bought her a wardrobe and she put her clothes in it.

Eventually she went to bed. In the morning she looked around her new room. Her wardrobe was gone! Daisy climbed out of her bed and walked into her parents' room. 'Mum, Dad, have you seen my wardrobe?' Daisy asked quietly.

'No dear, we haven't,' Mum answered.

Daisy was about to go downstairs when she saw her wardrobe at the bottom of the stairs. She couldn't believe her eyes! She ran back upstairs and told her mum and dad. They took the wardrobe back into Daisy's room.

The next night, Daisy stayed up all night. Every minute she looked at the wardrobe but suddenly it was gone! She looked downstairs and there it was. Suddenly, *crash!* The wardrobe fell down the stairs and all her clothes were scattered all over the floor. Daisy's parents came rushing out of the bedroom. They both said, 'Oh well, your clothes will have to stay on the floor in future.'

Daisy was the only girl in her school allowed to have a messy room!

Ashley Kirk (9)
North Primary School, Southall

The Mysterious Voice

Suzy was a young girl who lived in England. When Suzy was about nine years old her grandfather, who she was very close to, passed away. Her family went to her grandmother's to be with her for the funeral and lend support.

The family was upset and were still in shock. That night, after everybody had gone to bed, Suzy was still upset about her grandfather's death so she went to her grandmother's room and crawled into bed with her. Some time later that same evening Suzy awoke to a very faint male voice calling her name, 'Sssssssssssuzy.'

Suzy could feel coldness and fear rush over her. Grandma was sleeping so she thought her brothers must have called her in another room. Curious, she tiptoed to their room but they were both sleeping soundly. Confused, she checked on her parents, but they too were sleeping. She returned to her grandma's room and thought she must have imagined the voice after all, it had been a long day, and so she attempted to go back to sleep.

Before she could fall asleep she heard the voice again calling her name. 'Sssssssssuzy.' Now she was so scared she pulled the covers over her head and wished the voice would go away. After two or three more times of hearing this voice call her name and ignoring it, the voice grew louder. Suddenly an old man appeared whose legs were not on the ground and he was floating.

'Argh!' Suzy screamed loudly and ran off in fright.

Serena Sharma (11)
North Primary School, Southall

Tim And The Ghost

Once, long ago there lived a boy called Tim. Every night he would read a ghost story and never be scared. Everybody thought ghosts weren't real but Tim knew they existed.

The next day Tim had a terrible dream so he ran into his big sister's room and started crying, 'I … I.'

'Spit it out then,' said his older sister.

'I had a terrible dream that ghosts wanted to eat me alive.'

'But hang on a second you said you weren't scared of ghosts.'

'I know, it's never happened before.'

After that he kept having those dreams and he never found out why it happened, people said it was because a ghost haunted his room.

Tim never read ghost stories again!

Amber Bargota (9)
North Primary School, Southall

The Haunted House

One day after school Jack and his sister, Kate, couldn't wait till they got home because their dad had promised them that they could try out their new laptop. But on the way they got lost.

'Where are we?' questioned Kate, frightened.

'I don't know, Kate,' replied Jack nervously.

'I think we're lost,' panicked Kate.

They saw a house and they found the key.

'Shall we go inside?' exclaimed Jack excitedly.

'I don't think that is a good idea, Jack!' shouted Kate.

'It's only a quick look, anyway I don't think there's anyone inside, come on Kate,' Jack screamed.

So they decided to look inside the house which looked very haunted.

'Let's get out of here Jack!' yelled Kate.

'Why should we?' questioned Jack.

'Because it's spooky in here!' mentioned Kate.

'Fine then I'm going to look around, you can wait outside if you want,' said Jack rudely.

'Fine then I will!' screamed Kate loudly. So Kate waited outside while Jack looked inside the house.

He thought it was spooky too but he was brave enough to look inside.

'Ohhhhhhhh!' said a voice coming from nowhere.

'Come out wherever you are, show yourself!' yelled Jack.

'Ohhhhhh!' said the voice again.

Jack saw a ghost, he though he was just seeing things but he saw another ghost. This time he was frightened! Could he escape?

'Wake up Jack, it's time for school!' screamed his mum.

Jack went to school and told his friends.

Olivia Willetts (9)
North Primary School, Southall

The Haunted Cottage

The three friends had rented the cottage for the summer. The horrendous storm had been brewing for days, and when it finally came, it shook the whole earth and cracked it. The power of the storm was so mighty it felt like the dilapidated cottage would crumble.

Abnormal happenings had occurred at different times during the holiday, but they tried not to let these things spoil their fun. They thought it was their vivid imaginations playing up on them.

On the night of the storm however, it was revealed that they were not alone in the house. The friends could hear the sound of a baby crying and the eerie echo of a woman wailing. With the storm howling outside and the slates on the roof clattering, the friends could hear their hearts pounding like a drum and made their way to where the noise appeared to be coming from. They pushed open the creaky door of the upstairs room. The hairs on the back of their necks stood up and they trembled with fear. In the corner of the room they could see two shadowy creatures, and what they were about to witness would haunt them for the rest of their lives.

Daniel Kelly (11)
Our Lady & St Oswald's Catholic Primary School, Oswestry

The Ghost Ship

It was spring, when my class went away for a week's holiday. We all climbed into the bus, full of excitement and anticipation. It was the first time we would be staying away from home together.

We went on a night walk. It was pitch-black. It was cold and windy, in fact it was so windy you could lean back and the wind would keep you up! The walk took us along a beach. There was a thick mist coming off the sea.

I thought I saw an unusual shape in the mist. It looked like a ship that was sinking; I could see what I thought was its bow rising up from the water. There appeared to be people dangling from the metal railings. I could hear shouting and screaming, people calling for help. The mist was getting thick, I noticed the tide was coming in. I shouted but no one replied. While I was looking at the ship, my friends must have walked on. The tide at this point was touching my feet. I panicked and ran over the thick stones. I collapsed clutching my ankle.

I got up and continued to run. When I caught up with my friends, I was panting with fear. No one had seen the ship or had heard the people screaming. I wondered if it was just my imagination.

When I went to bed that night, the images I had seen and the screams I had heard, haunted my dreams all night.

Cian Jones (11)
Our Lady & St Oswald's Catholic Primary School, Oswestry

The Darkness Of Night

A long, long time ago, at Maeserfield, there was a haunted house on the top of a hill. The house was known as 'The House of Horrors.' The house was very dark with old window shutters that blew open and shut making loud squeaking noises.

Tiles were missing from the roof and the garden was very overgrown. There were big black iron gates at the front of the house with a long winding drive.

Inside the old house lived lots of rats, mice and bats who all made their own haunting noises. There were the largest cobwebs you had ever seen with over two hundred spiders. There were old paintings on the wall with eyes that seemed to follow you. Old furniture was covered in white dustsheets, which looked like ghosts in every room.

A young family bought the house and decided to make it their home. A few months after all the workmen had finished cleaning up the place the Stowell family moved into their new home.

After school, one afternoon, the oldest son called Simon was playing on his PlayStation game called *Medal of Honour*, when he heard a scream from the top floor! He slowly crept upstairs and, with sweat running down his neck, he opened the door. He could not believe his eyes, before him stood St Oswald himself in full armour.

'Simon, get up, you'll be late for school!' called him mum. It had all been a dream.

Connor Maguire (10)
Our Lady & St Oswald's Catholic Primary School, Oswestry

A Ghostly Feeling

I was sitting on my bed one day when all at once I felt the room go cold. Feeling what seemed like an icy cold peer on my back. I turned around to find nothing. Nothing but my bedroom wall. The walls which were once covered in posters and pictures were now bare. Suddenly I felt them closing in on me and then I felt sick but eventually must have fallen asleep.

When I awoke I found myself sitting on what seemed like the highest mountain in the world. Everything around me was pure white. I did not recognise this place, it was beautiful.

I was looking around at the calm and peacefulness when suddenly a glimmering person, a man, was standing in front of me. He then said, 'You will be safe up here, no one can hurt you again.'

'Again, what do you mean?' I said. 'Where am I?' But the glimmering shine just disappeared. I then realised where I was. I must be in Heaven, but why? Would I spend the rest of my life here? I then drifted back off to sleep.

Drowsily, I opened my eyes again, my whole body feeling like a lead weight. I could see all my wonderful toys and bedroom posters. Sitting up I felt as though someone was beside me stroking my arm. Was it my imagination or was there a ghost in my room? I shuddered a little but sat calm and realised I was not at all afraid.

Zoë Davies (11)
Our Lady & St Oswald's Catholic Primary School, Oswestry

The Valley

I looked over at the dilapidating valley across the street from my bedroom. It was quite a quiet street with a bunch of old shops and houses. It was dark and I could already see the moon hiding behind the clouds, I looked closer into the darkness. Two ghostly figures appeared into the darkness, I blinked, they were gone.

After school, I set off home with my friend Conan and we headed to my place. We went into my garden and after that we played on the PlayStation and I beat him.

Conan looked out the window and exclaimed, 'Let's go over there!'

I nodded excitedly. I had forgotten all about the night before and it sounded brilliant. We ran outside, and just at that moment, I felt a chill going down my spine, as the searing wind pierced my skin. As I ran down the street with Conan, we came to a halt. As we came to the dark valley that we'd stood in before. We both took a brave step into the darkness and almost instantly we were plunged into despair. The moon shone its gloomy light and the shadows inched their way towards us. Conan started to cry for help, and then an almost ear-splitting scream was heard out of the darkness. Two white hands reached out and grabbed us and we both screamed, then darkness. And how do I know all this? All the terror and tyranny? Because it was me!

Tobie Clarke (10)
Our Lady & St Oswald's Catholic Primary School, Oswestry

Now You See It ... Now You Don't

Eeeeek, went the cellar door, as I surreptitiously opened it. I crept down the stone steps, into the dusty wine cellar. Saw nothing at first until my eyes had adjusted to the murky light. Then I became aware of an iridescent sight.

I could see strange cartwheels, apparently moving on a road, and I could hear ghostly hooves moving in time with the wheels. I stood stock-still, and watched the drama unfold. Then I saw a child running with his hoop and joyfully laughing, with not a care in the world.

The scene unfolded before my hypnotic gaze. Suddenly out of the murk and the dust came an awful sight, it was a hunchbacked man, with a gruesome face, with horrible warts and very crooked teeth, this frightened the child intensely, and not to mention me who was watching the drama.

The child was so afraid of the man, he let out an alarming scream, which upset the ghostly horses, they then started to rear on their hind legs, they then started to run amock.

I was still frozen in a frightened trance, almost like my feet were glued to the floor. A red glow started surrounding me when the eyes of the spirits turned towards me, with a red frenzied stare. They all started to gang up on me, even the little boy, when suddenly the horses and cartwheels started to charge. The boy and hunchbacked man went under the wheels. Everything was normal in the cellar ...

Hollie Jones (11)
Our Lady & St Oswald's Catholic Primary School, Oswestry

Ghostly Goings On In Hawthorp Hotel

The lights flickered sending shadows soaring across my bedroom ceiling. I knew that there was someone around but I was too frightened to confront them. The floorboards gave a loud creak, and the door slammed shut.

'Is someone there?' I whispered. The curtains blew open and the mobile hanging on the ceiling started spinning.

I felt a cold hand on my shoulder, the hairs on the back of my neck stood up. I cried for help but nobody heard me. It was such a stormy night, the wind howled outside and the rain lashed against my window causing an old oak tree branch to tap on my window eerily.

I could also feel the breath of the person who was standing by my bed. It was terrifying. I was too scared to shout for my parents, in case it tried to hurt me. At this moment my heart was pounding. I couldn't turn the lights back on because it would hear me. A tear started to trickle down my cheek because I was so scared.

It grabbed me, took me out and dragged me downstairs, I couldn't shout because it had tied a piece of scarf around my mouth. Mum was in the living room watching TV and she came rushing out because she'd heard footsteps. She shook me and tried to wake me up, I was lying on the cold floorboards unconscious, what had it done to me? Lying there, right beside me, was a knife. Mum screamed!

Bethany Griffiths (11)
Our Lady & St Oswald's Catholic Primary School, Oswestry

The Boat Ghost

Late at night a boy ran through the docks shouting, 'Ghost! Help me, save me!' He ran on the ship, the sailors rushed to see what was the matter. They barged on board to find the boy curled up in the corner rocking himself gently. He screamed, 'Help me. It wants to kill me!' The sailors could not see the ghost.

Then cuts appeared from nowhere, there were cuts on his back and on his face, his arms and legs. The men picked him up and put him in a bed. That night the boy woke. Suddenly he saw the ghost, it stabbed him ten times, the boy wept and screamed. Although he did not die he was in pain. Soon he realised that he could not die from this ghost.

The next morning he climbed the mast and shot himself. He remained up in the mast. Soon the sailors looked for him on the ship and finally found him dead. They took him down and wrapped him up in his hammock.

That night the ghost came out and dragged the boy, it left a blood trail. The ghost woke. 'Now he's dead, he must be forgotten!' and left him. The sailors saw the note and the boy they knew was a ghost. Soon they all died except the captain ...

Christian Strandoo (10)
SS Peter & Paul CE (VA) Primary School, Eye

Welcome ... Goodbye

Far out in Australia, deep into the country was an old farmhouse and its owners were Fred and George.

Now let me tell you about my background, I was found in a box, as a ghost, and I don't know why but Fred and George called me Yoldemort. They thought it was appropriate for me.

You might think that is scary but it isn't. I'm friendly and kind. Most people are scared of me but I'm scared of two things. Fred and George's families and the box! I was scared because they were emigrating to us for at least a year.

I never felt so bad in my life, I let out the longest and loudest ghost moan I have ever done in my life. Suddenly there was a high-pitched scream as loud as mine! I shuddered. They had arrived.

I set out to greet them, more like send them back, when Fred stopped me in my tracks. 'Where are you going?' he demanded. I didn't reply. 'Back into the cellar!' roared Fred. I obeyed.

I thought I could slip out in the night-time but Fred was patrolling the rooms. Eventually I managed to freak Fred's gran out. She had a heart attack and they left. After that they never came back.

Henry Saunders (11)
SS Peter & Paul CE (VA) Primary School, Eye

Fresh Start

One day it was a fresh start for me because I moved house, but the best thing about it is that I had a bigger bedroom.

It was becoming dark and I went to bed because I was getting tired so I went up to my room. I was getting into my bed when suddenly the window burst open, so I went to close it when I heard a voice saying ... 'Help, help me get out!' So I just got into my bed and fell asleep.

I woke up at midnight and I heard crying again so I went downstairs and *smash, crash* there was a ghostly white figure throwing things. It caught sight of me and it stopped and said, 'Can you help me?' It was a ghost.

The moonlight was gleaming right through it, I began to help it. It wanted me to go down the cellar, so I grabbed a torch and followed the ghost.

It wanted me to get its body out of the wall. It said it had been murdered and bricked into the wall. It wanted me to get it out because it wanted to be buried by its family. So I got an axe, smashed the wall down and the body fell out. Then suddenly the ghost grabbed me and bricked me up in the wall and left me to die.

Ben Wade (11)
SS Peter & Paul CE (VA) Primary School, Eye

A Sleepover Nightmare!

'Why do penguins avoid the computer?' I asked.

'Because they don't want to be caught in the Internet!' Annie cried.

It was my birthday and I was having a sleepover. I had four of my friends there. We were just going to bed when we heard a *crash!*

We gasped. I gingerly pulled back my curtains. I screamed! A white face was staring back at me.

I lay awake for what seemed like ages, then finally I fell asleep ...

Eleanor entered first, then Orla, Annie and me. We waded through puddles of water until finally we saw a lamp. Dimly lit and shining, like the moon, was a face.

Orla held out her hand, 'Pleased to meet you, um ...'

'Boris is the name, trying to escape is my game!'

The wind howled and the motorway buzzed.

'I've been trapped up 'ere for years,' he groaned. I want to escape but I can't find the way!'

'Left, rig ...' began Eleanor.

'No!' interrupted Boris. 'I have to eat to get out. Eat flesh!'

'Aaaarrrrggghhhh!' we screamed.

'Flesh!' he screeched and glided across our heads. He blocked the way out!

My heart was beating, sweat was dripping down my forehead, then somebody shook me. 'Am I alive?' I whispered.

'What?' cried Eleanor.

'You've been dreaming!' Orla whispered.

Saskia Martindale (11)
SS Peter & Paul CE (VA) Primary School, Eye

The Haunted Forest

I was out one night camping with my dad in Thetford Forest.

It was Christmas Eve; the moon was glinting through a gap in the tent. I woke up and grabbed my bag, I strolled off into the trees, my eyes caught a glimpse of a lake and I slowly walked to a clearing where the lake was. I could see the reflection of the moon. Then I saw a reflection of another object I was too scared to look up. I slowly lifted my head, I froze, there was a green wrinkly old man, standing on the other side of the lake.

I slowly walked backwards. I turned and started to run back to my tent. The shadows of the trees lurked over me, my heart started to race, *thump, thump, thump!* I burst through my tent and zipped it up. My heart started to decrease in speed. I woke my dad up and told him what had happened; he grabbed the stuff and shoved it into the back of the car. As we climbed into the car, the monster burst through the trees, we sped off down the road. The ghost stood at the side of the road filled with anger.

And until this day the green old man chases all who trespass on his burial ground. I was lucky, I didn't meet his old friends in the heart of the Haunted Forest.

Conor Kavanagh (11)
SS Peter & Paul CE (VA) Primary School, Eye

The Old Fairground

My name is Billy and I live in London with my dad. We live right next to the great old famous fairground, which is supposed to be haunted.

We quite often used to sit and look out of the window across the fairground and often saw strange things.

One evening my dad and I decided that we would go for a walk through the fairground to see what we could find. It had got quite late and we had just decided it was time to go home, when we suddenly saw a ghost. He was very tall, dressed in black and didn't look very friendly. He was walking towards us staring at us all the time. We looked around to see how we should escape and noticed that there were more and more ghosts appearing. They were starting to form a gang and looked as though they were thinking about attacking us!

My dad said that we should hurry up and get out of there. I shouted to my dad that I had seen a movie once and if we killed the leader, the rest of them would leave us alone and we could escape.

I reached inside my pocket and found my penknife. I threw it as hard as I could and closed my eyes ...

Ben Chase (11)
SS Peter & Paul CE (VA) Primary School, Eye

Guest Room Ghost

1899:

My eyes were half open. My mother and my doctor stood at the end of my bed talking; they had not realised I had woken.

'... So I am afraid to say Mrs Pollson, Amy only has about two days left,' Doctor Higgins said grimly. 'But isn't there anything ... ?

'No, I'm afraid not Madam!'

There was silence as my mother stood there, pale and ummoving. I closed my eyes and ... died.

1918:

I was standing outside the guest room of our house above the Black Stallion - my parents being the owners of this pub. 'Come on Thomas, let's go,' my sister Susan was trying desperately to bring me away from the room. A freezing draught was blowing through the gap under its door. Ben our Collie dog was growling. Heckles of fur rose from his neck - just like before when we first explored this house. It was odd he'd never acted like this anywhere else in the house, and they say dogs can sense things we humans can't - spooky!

My mind turned back to old Mr Bentley from across the road. 'You need to be careful of that room, it's haunted. Many a time have I seen a ghostly white face of young Amy Pollson peering at me through that very window,' he said, pointing at the window of the guest room. 'Died of some illness ... lovely girl. Shame, shame!'

Afraid though I was, my curiosity got the better of me. I neared the door, turned the handle and pushed it open ...

Emily Jordan (11)
SS Peter & Paul CE (VA) Primary School, Eye

The Ghost Of My Family

I was sitting at my desk doing my homework. I heard a weird noise, but I thought I was hearing things, so I carried on. My mum called me to say dinner was ready, so off I went to get my dinner.

'Annalise would you like some tomato with your salad?'

'Yes please.'

Once I had finished my dinner, I went to finish my homework and go to bed. As I was about to go to sleep there was a noise coming from outside. I looked outside and there was nothing there, there was no noise and, as I went back into bed, the noise started again. I left a very heavy teddy on the bed and went over to the window, I saw loads of ghosts!

Then something caught my eye, Mum, Dad, Mickey (my brother) little Fifi (my baby sister). All, yes ... ghosts, my whole family dead, ghosts. I ran into my sister's room, nothing there, my brother's the same, and then my parents' room was the same.

Then I had a plan, I got dressed, put my shoes on and went into the garage. My dad had taught me how to drive a motorbike. I started it up, put the helmet and gloves on, opened the garage door and zoomed off.

Lauren Thomson (10)
SS Peter & Paul CE (VA) Primary School, Eye

A Ghost Story

It was always cold in that basement. As I descended the dank steps into the eternal darkness a cold breeze brushed against my shoulders. My father had always forbidden me from entering that place. 'It's dangerous down there,' he used to say. 'The steps are treacherous and one could easily fall and break his or her back.'

But I had disobeyed him. I had waited until he had gone to the store to pick up my mother and then I had crept stealthily to the landing and started down the dark, dingy stairwell to the misty abyss beyond.

I had lived in that small semi-detached house my whole life, my parents were hard-working folk who were typical parents. Only every so often my father would call in sick for work, go out and when he came back in the evening he would go down to the basement without a word. I always wondered what he did down there, and now I was going to find out. I reached the bottom of the steps and what I saw filled my heart with terror. I felt the icy hand of death around my throat and fell into unconsciousness.

Tom Taylor (13)
St Benedict's High School, Whitehaven

Killer Kaninchen!

She killed my rabbit, my wife had killed my rabbit. 'What did Fluffy ever do to anyone?' I cried like a banshee to my wife.

'Shut up about that revolting old rabbit,' my wife snapped back with unexpected venom.

'Why are you being like this dear?' I meekly whimpered back.

'I'm going to bed!' she bellowed.

'OK,' I said, whimpering again.

As my wife left the kitchen a silhouette jetted along the cold cobbled floor behind her. 'What the? Must have been a trick of the light.' Right away, after saying that, I followed the cold cobbles until I got to the warm, wonderful, luxurious carpet stairs. I climbed them all the way to the bedrooms on the mysteriously cold ground floor. I walked to my bedroom and switched on the light.

'Hi, darling,' I said cheerfully, but there was no reply. I crept over to the edge of her side of the bed. 'Noooo!' I screamed, she was dead! I could clearly see she had something protruding from her mouth. It was rabbit hay! As I stepped away from the horrific scene I knocked something over. It was a bottle of poison!

'Add 3 drops to a rabbit's hay' the label said clearly. Then I realised my rabbit's ghost had taken its revenge!

Niall McCormick (13)
St Benedict's High School, Whitehaven

The Ghost In My Bed

I got into bed then switched off the light ready to sleep. My dreams are always peaceful, but tonight they were full of dread of the mysterious unknown.

As I slept I felt the coldness of the world seep into my mind. My dream was that of an enormous manor that towered above me like a knife ready to strike. It was dark, so dark, that only the manor seemed to glow in the night.

I walked up to the large stained oak doors and knocked upon it. The door slid open by itself and a loud, but deathly creak admitted itself into the creepy atmosphere of the doorstep. The inside was furnished very differently from your normal manor. The walls were stained with blood and the floor was a light oak.

My brother appeared before me, but he was dead. I ran and followed him up some old stairs. When I got to the top I found the light switch for that floor. I pushed the switch and a dim light illuminated the room. My brother was there, he grabbed me.

I woke up in my bed dripping with sweat and there, right next to me, was my brother holding my hand and in the other hand a knife, saying, 'You left me.' I screamed, but no one could help me now.

Tom Kelly
St Benedict's High School, Whitehaven

Who?

It was dark, cold and silent. Only the wind blew through the trees making a quiet rustling sound. I sat on my bed waiting. But what for? I heard it again, that small child's voice. It was haunting my mind. Rushing through my head like a thousand knives stabbing into my brain. A huge bang came from the loft. I knew it was time. My nan had left me and my little sister the house in her will and told me that at 3am 'It happens'.

'What happens?'

She told me, 'At 3am they awaken and move everything.'

Bang! The bedroom door slammed shut. The lights flickered and I saw them! It was a figure of a small child and an adult, they stood at the doorway chanting. Coming closer and closer they repeated, 'Murder is sin,' over and over again. They sharply gazed into my eyes. The light went out and the room was in darkness. The window burst open and the wind howled and moaned, I ran and closed it as fast as I could. I reached for the light switch and flicked on. The room was empty.

In the centre of the room lay a photograph. It had a small child and an adult on it. It was them. On the back it had a faint outline saying 'Paula and Margaret'. But how had this mysterious picture got there? Who were Paul and Margaret? And why did they haunt this very house?

Jessica Harris (11)
St Chad's Catholic High School, Runcorn

Howling Calls

Upon a hilltop stood an old crooked building; with huge stained glass windows and leaning trees surrounded it. Living inside this strange house lived the Wokney family. Mum Lisa, Dad Mark, Rachel and Luke their children and Scurry the dog who had been their pet for years.

The family was sitting down watching television when suddenly there was a house-shaking bang on the door. As soon as the children heard it, it sent a shiver down their spines telling them that there was going to be trouble. Their mother's friend, Claire, arrived at their doorstep. Out of nowhere the sky turned a dark denim-blue as drops started thumping down, drumming on the quick, swaying grass. 'Claire is *here!'* murmured the children. Claire asked if she could stay for the night. Lisa agreed.

The night seemed to have dragged on afterwards. Finally it was time for bed so everyone stumbled up the stairs into their rooms. As Scruffy plodded on along behind them, a white figure wandered into Scruffy and made him start to feel strange and want to be nasty. Then for some reason Scruffy did not go to his basket, he went into another room, but he did not realise. As Claire sank down into her mattress, she heard a wild howl under her bed ... she paused ... but before she could look, a hairy tatty animal was stood, growling in her face!

The next morning Claire never came down for her breakfast and the dog was feeling ill ...

Shannon Miller (12)
St Chad's Catholic High School, Runcorn

The Girl Alone In The Swimming Baths ...

As she was walking through, it wasn't that bad at first, but as it grew darker, she was petrified.

Lucy kept telling herself that nothing was going to happen, but she felt small drops of water tapping onto her nose, it was raining ...

The rain was now beating down hard all over her body, she scrambled into her school bag and pulled out her fleece jacket, but that didn't stop her from getting drenched.

Suddenly a black ghostly shadow hovering on the dark pathway appeared, it leapt forward grabbing Lucy and knocking her unconscious ...

Three hours later Lucy woke, feeling dizzy and dazed. She was damp all over, cold and empty. As she sat up, she went into deep panic, everywhere was ghost-like. She was in some derelict swimming baths.

She stood up and looked around. She was by the poolside. She saw flakes of mould on top of the pool water and there was a terrible stench. Blood splattered up the wall tiles and a rusted lifeguard's deckchair knocked over by the poolside ...

Naiomi Dean (12)
St Chad's Catholic High School, Runcorn

Supper's End

In the eerie moors of Wales a man sat in his house worrying. Napoleon was on the verge of invading Great Britain. He had been in the army and hadn't trusted it since.

'Junior, Betty, go to bed,' the man said. The children sighed and put down the doll they had been fighting over and went to their rooms. The man took a smoke of his pipe. *Aah, finest in the country,* he thought.

The children started crying in their rooms. *It's nothing,* he thought. It would be supper soon. The man was craving for his favourite. Sardine sandwiches and a glass of brandy.

'Wife, how's the supper coming?'

'Argh!' A blood-curdling scream came from the kitchen.

'Wife, you better not have broken my favourite mug,' he shouted. *Handgun, just in case ...* he thought. He slowly walked up to the wooden pantry door holding his gun in a quivering hand.

Crack! The head of an axe came through the pantry door. 'Supper's been cancelled,' said a scratchy voice.

Crack! Bang!

Ben Clarke (11)
St Chad's Catholic High School, Runcorn

The Hallowe'en Nightmare

It was 7.30, already dark because of the clocks going back. Andrew was walking home from a friend's house down the side of the canal. For some reason Andrew paid a lot of attention to the canal this time. It seemed more frightening. Maybe it was just the fact it was Hallowe'en had something to do with it. Andrew was not the type of boy to be easily scared. In fact he was the opposite, a strong, fearless and courageous character. The thought that he was alone lay heavy on his mind though. That's probably why everything seemed so different and spooky this time. Andrew also feared death badly which shouldn't occur at 13. Andrew finally came to where the path split.

Andrew normally would take the path left but this time curiosity got the better of him when he saw a spot of light. Andrew reached the light although he didn't yet know where it was coming from.

Then the light went out. Andrew was really scared now. He took a couple of steps back.

Out of the corner of his eye he could make out a grey figure rising out of the water. He daren't look but the temptation was too much. As soon as he made eye contact with the figure it began to talk, its words were: 'Run child run!' and then just a lot of screaming and moaning. Then he awoke at the exact spot. Was it a nightmare or real? He'll never know.

Anthony Fisher (12)
St Chad's Catholic High School, Runcorn

The Doll

It all started last week, I was in the pub and a man came up to me. I couldn't see his face, because he was wearing a jet-black cloak and he had the hood up. He said, 'Would you like a game of cards?'

I replied, 'Yes I would.'

So we went over to a table in a dark corner. The card game was Black Jack, I won.

Then the man said, 'For winning, I will give you this.' The man pulled out from the depths of his pocket, a doll made out of twigs, hay and a nut. After I had finished examining the doll I went to look at the man, but he had vanished.

Later that night I couldn't get to sleep because the wind was howling. Then, *crash!* A plate had just fallen in the kitchen. Then my CD player turned on in the living room. It was on repeat all night. Then once the sun shone through the window, it stopped. This carried on for two days. Then, when it happened on the third day, I went down to the kitchen. I opened the door a tiny bit and there was the doll walking round with a flame torch making plates smash by heating them up. But there was something different about the doll, it had eyes and a mouth. Then I sneezed. The doll spotted me and said, 'You!' Then it started to run at me. Then the sun shone through the window. I was saved. I threw away the doll that morning.

Steven Craig (11)
St Chad's Catholic High School, Runcorn

The Town That Never Was

John was walking quickly through the forest. His car had broken down. It was raining heavily. He quickened his pace through the forest. He tripped over a log, straight into a pile of mud. He looked up and wiped his face. There was a man standing there. The man said, 'You need to dry off, come with me.'

Even though John didn't know this man he trusted him. John said to the man, 'Can I have some petrol? my car's broken down.'

The man said, 'Yes, but you have to go to the shop for it.'

The money was different than normal money, so John kept a coin from the change from the petrol - he gave the change back to the man and said, 'Goodbye.'

The man said, 'Good luck, come back if you can.' John rushed back through the forest to his car.

On the way out of the forest John noticed that a sign said, *Welcome To Spectre.* John ignored it and drove home. At home there were two policemen sitting with his wife. She looked like she had been crying. She said, 'I thought you were missing.'

John told the police where he was, but they didn't believe him so he took them to the forest. John looked for the sign, but it was covered in ivy like it had been left for ages and the town wasn't there. It was just a graveyard. John said, 'I swear, I'm not lying.'

Then the police said, 'Yeah, OK we believe you, let's go.'

In the car on the way home John felt something hard in his pocket. He put his hand in his pocket and pulled out the coin. There was a picture of the town and the motto was 'you never knew we were there'.

Amy Chatten (12)
St Chad's Catholic High School, Runcorn

The Haunting

When I was small my nan told me a story. The tale goes like this: in a little village in Wales, mysterious disappearances were happening. Children, adults, cats and dogs, all were drawn to a derelict house and were never seen again.

My nan and her friends decided to go camping not far from the large house, they set up camp feeling excited but also a little scared of the night ahead.

They were surrounded by trees. They had all settled down in their sleeping bags. Everyone except my nan had fallen asleep. It was around 12 o'clock, she kept hearing strange noises and flashing lights from inside the tent. She was brave enough to open the zips of the tent slowly and step outside. The night was dark and gloomy, there was fog throughout the whole sky. It was everywhere, she followed a path which led up to the door of the foreboding-looking house, it was as if some spirit had guided her there.

Back at the tent everyone was awakening to a shrill scream, they followed the echo of the scream, all huddling together in fear. They approached the house and were surprised to see that the large front door was wide open. On the stairs by the cellar there was a very tall, white, ghostly figure beckoning them all to come forward. They all approached the cellar steps not wanting to go down there, but they did. They were drawn down there by the same thing Nan had experienced. Down there were stuffed figures of people, animals, they wanted to run but couldn't, something had hold of them, they could not get away.

My nan had pulled herself away from the strength of the presence of the ghostly figure and had managed to escape. She never saw her friends again from that night onwards.

So did her friends die or does life still go on at the old derelict house in Wales or not? You make up your own mind ...

Ashleigh White (12)
St Chad's Catholic High School, Runcorn

My Nightmare

I woke up late this morning. *Wonder why Mum didn't wake me?* When I went downstairs Mum wouldn't talk to me. She wouldn't even make my breakfast. She made my brother's breakfast, she even gave him a hug, but not me. What had I done to upset her so much?

I got my coat and my bag but still she wasn't talking to me. Then I went out. She got in the car with my brother and went without me. Funny though, I don't remember *that* car. Where's our normal car?

Took myself to school but no one wanted to talk to me. Lunchtime was strange too, I asked Naiomi with Terri and Chloe. They kept whispering, I'm sure they were talking about me.

When I got home Mum still was not talking to me. She was playing with my brother, so I went upstairs to my room. I think I'll have a nap until Dad gets home. He always calls me his angel. I know he'll talk to me.

Woke up, it's six o'clock. Dad should be home by now. I walked downstairs and into the living room, there's Dad with Mum. They're both crying and I don't know what's wrong.

'I can't believe she's gone,' cried Mum.

'How did this happen to my angel?' cried Dad.

Now I understand, now I remember my nightmare, the crash, the screaming, the new car - it's me, I'm gone, I'm dead.

Kira Cummins (11)
St Chad's Catholic High School, Runcorn

The Ghost Janitor

It had just turned four o'clock and I had a detention with Mr Coyle. I had to sit and write for a whole hour. Mr Coyle finally said, 'You may leave.' So I picked up my bag and left the classroom. I walked through a dark corridor with only a little beam of light.

I could see a ghostly figure of a man, who looked like a janitor. 'Hello,' I said, he looked at me with bright yellow eyes. 'Are you the school's janitor?' I said nervously. He nodded. So off I walked into the dark, gloomy night. On the way home the bright moon shone in my eyes, and then a thin layer of fog rose from the ground. I ran home really scared.

I couldn't get to sleep that night, I couldn't stop thinking of that man. *Did he have a name? How come he never talked to anyone?* I thought to myself.

The next day I met my friend Alex at the shop. 'Last night was really strange, he had bright yellow eyes!'

'Who?' questioned Alex.

'Our school's janitor.'

'Tom,' said Alex nervously, 'our school's janitor died last week and we haven't had one since.'

Tony Dainteth (12)
St Chad's Catholic High School, Runcorn

The Hallowe'en Ghost

It was Hallowe'en night, a dark and windy night. A boy named tom woke up in a pitch-black room. Tom was scared, he was wondering how he'd got there and where he was.

Tom heard something heavily breathing not that far away from him. He shouted, 'Who's there?'

A reply came back, 'My name is George.'

Tom asked, 'Can you find the light switch?'

'Yes it's here, I'll put the light on now!'

The lights from above flickered on, Tom could now see a small man tucked up in the corner of the room. It looked like an old bathroom. Tom knew he and the man were trapped.

In the middle of the floor was a ring that looked like it was burnt out. Tom tapped on it, it was hollow. Next to it, was a large sledgehammer. Tom had a thought, suddenly he picked it up and hit it against the floor. He fell down into something that looked like a well.

Tom was now worried, he was stuck down there, bubbles started to rise to the top of the water. Suddenly a pale, deformed-looking girl jumped out of the water, grabbed Tom and tried to rip the flesh off of his face ...

Joe Bibby (12)
St Chad's Catholic High School, Runcorn

The Quarters

John, Dylan and Lorna were all wondering how they had talked each other into such a dare, as to go down into Talon Hall's old servants' quarters. The ghost story about 'the old servant working alone and dying alone mysteriously' the night earlier had first given Dylan the idea to sway the other two into this treacherous predicament and the hitch of them never finding the servant's body only grew his enthusiasm further. But he didn't plan on John objecting and dragging him into it.

'Oh no, you're not getting us two into another one of your ridiculous dares alone. This time *you* have to do it too,' John had said.

'Fine!' Dylan began. 'I'll come on your little adventure, I wouldn't try and get either one of you two into something too scary for even me anyway. I'll meet *both* of you outside the bogs in the hallway. Agreed?'

'Agreed,' sighed John and Lorna.

Back in the story, all three were at the stairs leading to the servants' quarters.

'OK, on three,' started John with an obvious level of distress in his voice. 'One ... two ... *three!'* They all charged in, although hesitating in their minds ...

'And none of them were ever seen again,' ended one of the hall's workers, recounting the events of what had happened on that fateful night several years ago.

'Pssst!' whispered one of the young Year 7s to his friend. 'How about we go down there tonight and have a look around ...'

Callum Hough (13)
St Chad's Catholic High School, Runcorn

Darkness

Faster and faster I run, my heart pounding fiercely against my chest. It can't be happening, he can't be dead!

My legs have gone numb, surely I will be next. I've got to get away, find help, stay alive.

I trip on a headstone and fall to the ground. Time stops. Pitiful wailing fills the air, darkness takes over my body. The black smothers me, wraps me tight. I can't get out!

And then I'm back and he is with me too, we hold each other close and glide swiftly home.

As the days go by we watch the search parties go out. They find our bodies. We attend our funerals.

Our troubles are over now ...

Stephanie Darlington (13)
St Chad's Catholic High School, Runcorn

The 12 O'Clock Curse

It was 11.58 on a dark, stormy night and a man was reading a newspaper. It mentioned in the newspaper people had been mysteriously dying at bang on 12 o'clock at night. As he read, his big, old grandfather clock in the corner started to chime. It was 12 o'clock. Then suddenly after the clock struck for the twelfth time, he heard an agonising, blood-curdling scream. He jumped out of the chair and raced downstairs to meet a body lying on the floor in the kitchen with blood everywhere. Then he heard a muffled laugh. He was scared. He literally jumped on the phone and rang 999. Then all of a sudden he felt drowsy and dropped to the floor.

It was 11.58 again the following night and he was reading a newspaper about what had happened last night. Then the clock struck 12 and he heard that cackling laugh again. He started to run but all of a sudden stopped and fell to the floor, dead. But people in the area say they can still see a reading light on every night at 11.58.

Ryan Slater-Davis (13)
St Chad's Catholic High School, Runcorn

Extract From 'Seeing Is Believing'

'Hey, wait!' I exclaimed as I noticed Jake and Emma leaving down the hall without me. I had read enough horror stories and seen enough scary movies to know that being separated in a haunted house is not good.

As we continued down the hall I pondered what we would find in this so-called 'haunted' house. I mean, sure, people had died here, but could that really mean … ghosts?

Shaking my head, I took a deep breath. We needed to think logically and stay on one thought - finding an exit. Emma led the way in front, with Jake beside me. We suddenly stepped off the carpet and continued walking on a wooden floor. Our footsteps sounded oddly loud and I could hear the echoes. Was it just me, or were there other noises too? Was I imagining that clock ticking and the consistent dripping of a tap?

Tick-tock … drip, drip, drip … tick-tock … drip, drip, drip … To take my mind off these eerie noises, I concentrated on my surroundings. Bad idea. We passed a room with a door slightly ajar. Peeking in, I stifled a scream. It came out as more of a yelp. My friends spun around to glare at me.

'Never scare me like that *again!'* hissed Emma.

'Well sorry! But I think you'd scream!' I snapped back.

The room was a nursery. On the rug was a pool of blood. A small doll with dull, creepy, lifeless eyes and a dagger, were made crimson by the blood.

Sarah Steele (12)
St Chad's Catholic High School, Runcorn

Dreams

Two weeks had passed and there has still been no news on David. Since he's been away to war I have no hope any more. It's all gone.

Today, as always I woke up, trudged downstairs feeling my dressing gown trail behind me and my eyes feeling as heavy as a bag of bricks, switched on the TV and slouched on the couch like I do every day.

That's when I saw it.

My eyes hanging so heavy I thought I was seeing things. I blinked twice and it was still there. I looked back at the TV and there it was beaming across my eyes. A big news headline exclaiming, '20 British killed in tragic bomb accident'. My heart stopped. A picture of David lit up the screen.

I told myself I'm seeing things over and over again. That's when I realised he's gone. I'm never going to see him again.

Moments later I felt a cold shiver sprint up the spine of my back. A big, black shadow was standing over me.

I felt a hand touch the side of my face as I jumped out of bed. I saw David. I realised I must have been having a nightmare.

A loud bang at the door hurdled through my ears. As I went down to answer it I saw two men dressed in khaki green suits.

I suddenly realised it's just like my dream and now I have to go through all this again. But this time for real.

Laura Glass
St Hilda's CE School, Hartlepool

The Anniversary

It was a normal day and I was coming home, but I couldn't shake the feeling of apprehension.

I came to Old Cemetery Road to reach the headland where I live. I decided to try and tire myself out, so hopefully, when I go to sleep the horrifying dreams would not return.

As I made my way to Marine Drive the smell of sea salt grew stronger as I heard the sea crashing into the coast. A feeling of trepidation which would return later that night.

I began to run faster in the dark and lashing down rain across the moor, all of a sudden the ground crumbled, I began to spiral into the darkness.

I woke with a gasp looking around furiously, shaking with fear, I threw myself out of my bed crashing into everything. I opened my gran's door, she woke up with a start. I slowly tried to explain about these dreams I had been having. She said, 'Let's go downstairs and you can explain.' I finally brought myself round and explained to her about these nightmares. Her face showed concern and then understanding. She got up and searched in the cupboard returning with a newspaper yellowed with age. She said, 'I think you should have a look at this.' The newspaper read 'girl dies in tragic accident'! The article said how a young girl of the same age as me died when an old mine shaft caved in due to torrential rain on coming home from school. The name of the girl read the name of my gran, she explained that the girl was my grandad's sister, was this a warning?

The next day I went to school as usual. I walked home. Shortly before I reached the moor, it softly started to rain.

Cheryl Baxter
St Hilda's CE School, Hartlepool

The Masks

'Why did we pinch the masks? Why did they draw us to them? Why did they change us?'

'Shut up!' I whispered, my legs were getting cramp. We had been in that smelly cupboard for hours. We were after these voodoo masks for Hallowe'en out of the art room.

We came out of the cupboard and saw the masks, we wrapped them up and put them in our bags and made a dash for it. We were seen but not caught! But we dashed through the fire exit and ran for it. We met on the field behind my house. We revealed the masks and they put fear into me.

All of a sudden my mind started to spin and my brain bubbled, I tried to pull the mask off but it had stuck and turned see-through. A voice stated in my head, 'Kill, kill,' it whispered. It got louder and louder till I had to do as it said. The three of us set off on a murdering spree.

We set off down the back alley towards an abandoned warehouse killing all we found. By this time it was cold, wet and dark. As the sun popped over the hill tops, I awoke suddenly and the masks had come off when I awoke. We were horrified at what we had done. We went to the seaside and flung the masks in.

It was some weeks later that we heard that two young boys in Europe found the masks on a beach and what they did with them is a whole different story.

Alexander Morgan Cook
St Hilda's CE School, Hartlepool

Shadows In The Dark!

Abbie ran shivering with fear, it was him, yes him, the one that had killed her mother and father, every place she went he was there. She ran faster than ever until … *crash!*

Abbie had fallen into a pile of bin bags blocking the alleyway, leading towards the local supermarket. She jumped up quickly and ran. She ran inside the supermarket, a woman stopped her. 'Why so fast dear?' asked the puzzled woman. She looked back but he had gone, he was nowhere to be seen.

Abbie stayed put for a short while, just to be sure that she was never to see this person ever again.

Bethan Williams (11)
St Teresa's Junior School, Liverpool

The Mystery That Wasn't Solved

Bang!

'Argh what was that?' I said running the horrid staircase. As I ran one of the wooden planks snapped. Suddenly I heard, 'Mark,' in a very deep voice. 'Mark Brownlow.' It was coming from the toilet.

As I crept over to the toilet door I heard a noise upstairs, 'Nooo! there is two of them.'

'No Mark, there's only me,' this time from the kitchen.

'Who and where are you?'

'I'm Frank Marly and I am behind you …'

Jak Flanagan (11)
St Teresa's Junior School, Liverpool

The Ghost That Wanted To Rest

It all started when I was 9 years old, my sister and I went to school and it changed our lives. That day was just like any old schoolday. But there was something different, but we just could not work it out. Maybe it was just our imagination.

When we got home we said to our mum, 'We have been seeing things today, but it might have been the lights because they have been going on and off all day.'

In the night we kept on hearing noises so we got out of bed and there was a ghost. So we ran downstairs and told our mum, we all walked upstairs, but our mum could not see anything, but we still could. I looked at my sister and said, 'We must be the only ones that can see the ghost, because no one was getting bothered in class.'

Our mum said, 'Stop being silly.'

An hour later a girl appeared. She said, 'My stepmum always locked me in my room, and I fell out of my window. She told the police I ran away and she buried my bones outside your bedroom window, all I want is to rest.'

My sister and I ran downstairs and said to my mum, 'Mum, phone the police, there is a body outside our window.'

She phoned the police and the body was found. We never saw the ghost again.

Stephanie Macilwee (10)
St Teresa's Junior School, Liverpool

The Thing

Suddenly I fell to my knees. A shiver ran up my spine as I touched the cold floor. I felt a bony hand touch my shoulder. A croaky voice said, 'Don't turn round.' I got up. I ran. I ran as fast as I could through the dark forest, tripping over my own feet. My heart pounding. Sweat dripping off my feet. I could hear footsteps following me. They got faster, then they stopped, so did I. I could tell it was there behind me.

The voice said again, 'Don't turn round.'

I couldn't take it. I swivelled round slowly. To my amazement, there was nothing there, just leaves blowing in the breeze. Was it just me? Was it in my head? Was it a dream? It can't have been, it seemed so real.

I had one last look around and headed back home, my head hung low. Then I heard a sudden noise, a screeching sound. I looked up, turned around. It was there. The Thing. A big raging ball of fire flew up into the midnight sky. There was blood dripping down its face. It was so gruesome. The Thing. That's all I can say, I didn't know what it was. I was at death's door if I didn't run. I ran into my house, bolted the door and ran upstairs. It was so strong it just broke through. I looked into its eyes. Then I fell to the floor. Was I dead?

Emily Ingram (12)
South Holderness Technology College, Hull

House On The Hill

It was quiet in the Ghost Inc, but this was nothing new to Ben. He had no idea why he opened this place, it was just used as a joke, so far 5 in 6 of the calls they'd had this year were jokes, the sixth someone had the wrong number. Ben sat thinking of what his friends had told him before they went down to the river. 'Ben, I'm fed up with sitting around here,' Anth had said.

'We could be making money but just sit chucking out time we could use for fun,' Max had blurted out.

As they'd left, Ben had tried to reason with the twins, Dex and Jake, they'd tried to say, 'Just quit while you have a chance,' and closed the door. Ben was now just sat, no money, no life, no choice. He reached for the phone, to tell the others he'd made up his mind, when it started to ring. Ben would have begun to have hope at this point, but 6 calls with nothing to help, had taken away that hope. He picked up anyway, and before he could ask who was calling, a grief-stricken voice spoke, 'Hello? Please, help! It's coming, it knows me, it's in my mind, make it stop! It's near, near, me ...' Then the dial tone began to buzz. A joke or someone in danger? Ben had no idea, but his conscience told him this could be it, and someone was in danger, terribly deep in it to by the sounds of it. He wrote down the address and quickly called his friends.

It was now late, and the sky was a light purple colour, the only sounds were a few twittering birds, and the roar of the engine. Ben parked the van at the bottom of the street, and stared at the old mansion, a typical scene from a horror movie. Everyone clambered out, and grabbed their equipment, like heat-seeking cameras, night vision, charms and holy objects as a 'just in case'. They advanced on the towering building, not saying a word. Once they had approached, a man suddenly burst out the doors and stumbled towards them. 'Please, come see what it did!' He dragged them in, the sight was horrific. One girl laid with what looked like her hand sticking out of her mouth. A boy had been bent into impossible positions, with bones stuck through his bloodstained skin. And the other, it was impossible to tell what that pile of flesh was. As they stared, the man locked the door, and approached them, with a menacing grin. 'Now you're here, the fun will begin.' He pulled an axe out of the girl's skull, and charged the 5 friends. He struck Jake with a powerful blow, spraying blood everywhere.

The others ran in fear as the man threw the weapon at random, hitting Max's back. He fell, as the killer walked up, and dug the axe in deeper. The others ran into a dark room.

'He killed them!' yelled Anth hysterically.

'Shh, he'll hear us,' whispered Ben. 'Listen, that guy, he's been possessed, we need to get the thing out of him.'

'What?' yelled Dex. 'How can you just jump in and say he's possessed? You don't know that! You're the mad one!'

Ben was about to answer, when a blade shot through the wall Dex had his back to, somehow the heart was still beating, and on the end of the blade for show.

The maniac walked in, his bloody axe in hand, grinning. Anth ran at him, only to get hacked into pieces. Ben ran, but the freak threw the axe again catching Ben's foot. He fell, and the madman approached, he yanked out the axe, his eyes red - he was possessed! But before Ben could move, the axe struck him. The last thing he saw, was the axe inches from his neck.

Chris Harrison (13)
South Holderness Technology College, Hull

Devil Or Not?

One cold winter's night Abigail was walking in the snow kicking her feet, she heard a scream so she ran through the garden, up the stairs and into the house to see if she could help. She heard a growling noise coming from the kitchen so she peeked round the door to see a strange creature sitting on the table. It was huge and red, and was engulfed in red scales and knives. But its eyes said that it was frail and scared.

A floorboard creaked and it saw her, she ran and shot up onto the ceiling, it scattered into a mirror and disappeared. To this day the creature comes out every night at midnight. It is still in someone's house. Now could it be in yours?

Stephanie Nicholson (13)
South Holderness Technology College, Hull

The Contamination

It was a glorious summer's day. They were out playing football and one boy gave the ball an enormous whack and it flew through the window of the upstairs window of Haraldby Hall which everyone knew to be haunted. It was up to Jonny to fetch the ball.

As he walked up to the rusty, squeaking gates, lightning struck the top of the structure causing bats to shoot out the upstairs window. He was a little taken aback but he carried on through the massive stone doors. Around him he saw the foyer full of shattered tiles and what looked like great dark artefacts were spread about the area. He clambered up the stairs. This was a great staircase that went to the top of the building. He took it as far as it would go. There were many unspeakable things Jonny saw inside that wicked house that day.

When he reached the top floor he found the ball was perfectly placed in the centre of the room. He picked the ball up but as soon as he looked up he dropped the ball again. A great massive marble door stood there with glyphs and warnings all over it. Johnny rushed over and turned the handle. He had just brought a deadly curse upon the world.

Michael Wright (13)
South Holderness Technology College, Hull

The Killing

I could feel my heart slowing down as my life was being stolen from me. I spun around, my eyes coming into contact with a man's. His were blue, bright blue and full of hatred. Just cold.

As my body gradually became weaker, I studied the features of the man in front of me. His skin was warm, his hands were squeezing my neck. His hair was blond and short hanging over one eye. You're probably thinking, *his hair is normal,* but there was one thing that terrified me, his face - cut and scarred, like knife wounds. They looked fresh and were still open, bleeding ...

'Who are you?' I tried to yell, my voice a whisper.

'That's not important,' he replied, his accent was hard to place. 'What is important, is that you know you're going to die tonight.'

His voice made me shiver. It sounded like he had a French accent. Then I had an idea. I had to try to live!

'W-what's your name?' I stammered, hoping he wouldn't squeeze my neck harder. Then it all went wrong.

'You mock me ...' he whispered in my ear. The man pulled a gun from his coat and put it to my head ...

Sophie Parsonage (12)
South Holderness Technology College, Hull

The Family Spirit Never Dies

'Ruby, you will be late for school, hurry up.'

I wish that were you calling me. I wish you were all here. I lost you Mum when I was only young. I lost you all, my whole family that terrible night. I still have Grandma and Grandad but nothing like having my parents and sister.

I collect my bags and head downstairs. In the kitchen Grandma and Grandad are making breakfast. I am not hungry. I rush out the door before saying goodbye. I cannot stop thinking of you all.

I make my way through the leaf-covered autumn streets. I reach that house and again, like every morning, I stop and stare. The house is now deserted and covered in moss and cobwebs. I still remember everything.

Coming back from school, I feel I must enter this house again. My hands shake as I turn the old wooden handle and let myself in. An eerie chill surrounds me. The whole house begins to shake and old pictures fall from the walls. I run for the safety of my old room as an icy wind blows through my hair.

I know it is the spirits of my family, the family I lost.

'Ruby, don't be afraid. We love you and miss you, but we must leave this house now. Always remember we are with you. Remember the family spirit never dies.'

The three visions that had been there in my room vanished. I tried to reach them but my hands were left empty.

Rachel Argent (11)
South Holderness Technology College, Hull

A Story Never To Be Told Again

I stared up at the house as the gate opened. I walked along the path, I glanced at the graveyard to read the name of my mother, a tear dripped down my face. I knew we were moving, it was to get away from all the memories of Mum, but I didn't know we were moving into the haunted house.

The door opened by itself. As soon as we entered we heard creaks and groans and the lights started to flicker.

I ran upstairs. I hated this house. I hated Dad.

A girl came up to me and told me to leave or I'd be sorry. She was young, about my age and she looked strangely normal and scared. I was scared so I ran into the attic. I was suddenly drawn to a chest. It was covered in dust. I drew back the lid to find two photo albums just like the ones Mum used to have. I opened one to find pictures of the girl that was haunting us, only they were all in colour. I opened the second one to find black and white photos of my family. For the first time I looked at myself properly, I was transparent. I ran to the graveyard to find my own name engraved on a rock. I looked up to see my mum.

This was a story never to be told again. I was a ghost and I would be forever.

Rachael Fothergill (12)
South Holderness Technology College, Hull

Me

I was walking down the street on the way to my friend's house. I noticed this man was following me. I just ignored it and kept on walking. He was getting faster and faster, he kept gaining on me. I hid in a bush hoping he would go away and he did. Well I thought he did.

I came out and there he was. He put his hand around my mouth. I tried to scream but I couldn't, I was too scared. He dragged me into a valley. All of a sudden it all went black, my life flashed before my eyes. I felt him sticking a dagger in my back. I couldn't do anything, I was dying or was I already dead?

Hayley Addison (12)
South Holderness Technology College, Hull

Ghost Shoes

One night in October the leaves on the trees were rustling against the window. Becky shouted to her mum, 'Night,' she shut her door with a slam and went to bed. Later on she awoke with a *bang* then a *tap, tap, tap.* She approached her door and opened it slowly, it creaked.

It was her dad coming in from work. She crept downstairs hearing whispering and talking. She ran back to her room. She opened her bedroom door and saw the wardrobe open, and the pair of shoes her mum had bought her on her bed. She was shocked, scared and worried. She put them back in her wardrobe and went to bed.

She awoke early ran over and got the shoes and put them on her bed. She slowly took off the lid and said, 'They're just shoes made of leather and that's all.' Her mum shouted her downstairs for breakfast, when she went up the shoes were on her window sill and her pillows on the floor, rubbish was out of the bin, everywhere. She cried, her mum wondered what was wrong with her daughter.

Dad came running in. 'We are moving, we have 3 hours to pack.'

Becky thought to herself, *no, I'm not taking the shoes,* and threw them in the bin. They got in the car and started to drive away. Becky looked back and the shoes were scrambling at the window *trying to escape ...*

Sarah Miller (12)
South Holderness Technology College, Hull

The Girl In The Mine

'Beatrice? Don't run away from me. I don't know this mine as well as you do. Please.'

There it was again, that sobbing voice, those echoing footsteps behind her! Where was the rest of her tour group and her parents? Bea kept running - heart pounding, sweat sheeting down. When finally she looked round, she screamed. Behind her was a white figure, arms outstretched, shrieking desperately.

'Beatrice, please come to me.' At first she sounded human, but now her words were turning raspy and frightening.

'You can't hide from me, you can't hide, come to me, come to *meeeeeee*!'

Suddenly Bea saw a light! The mine gate - if she could just get there. And there it was, cold metal in her hands. She pushed it open, slamming it behind her. Bea looked back and saw a little girl with blonde plaits and a blue dress. Her eyes shone green in her pale face. She was crying.

'Please Beatrice don't leave me here again!' she said.

'I don't understand!' said Bea.

The girl sobbed once more and disappeared back into the mine.

Bea looked behind her and there was her tour! Her parents hadn't noticed she had gone. She slipped in at the back in time to hear her guide say, 'They say one of the girls from the village led young Mary Farthing into the mine for a joke. But she was never found and they never found out which girl did it.

'I know,' said Bea, 'it was Beatrice.'

Maud Morrish (12)
The Atherley School & Grove Place Preparatory School, Southampton

Not Wanted

There was a family of three. They lived in a flat in London but wanted to live somewhere bigger. One day their dad was looking through some papers for houses and saw a 31-bedroomed house in the country. He couldn't believe his luck. He went for the house.

The family soon moved in. On their first night, everyone was ecstatic and very pleased. It was everything they had ever wished for. They were all eating dinner joyfully. But their feelings were soon about to take a dramatic turn.

'Look Dad, the painting is moving,' Stacey exclaimed and sure enough the painting was gliding. Next minute the vase flew across the room and crashed against the wall. They all stood up. Suddenly the chandelier started swaying, the doors kept opening and shutting and the plates on the table fell off. They all ran into the kitchen. The plates and cutlery were all flying. As they tried to shut the cupboards the cutlery pointed at them. It started flying towards them. They ran out and shut the door. They heard the plates smash against the floor.

They ran upstairs to gather their stuff. They collected whatever they could lay their hands on then ran downstairs. As they were running, spooky noises erupted all around them. They kept running for their lives. The telephone was hovering in mid-air. They opened the door and ran. They were meant to be crying tears of happiness but instead were crying tears of horror.

Maninder Sahota (13)
The Atherley School & Grove Place Preparatory School, Southampton

The Midnight Tour

It was a cold night in January, our school had taken us on a trip in Yorkshire and we were doing a midnight ghost tour through a graveyard. We all thought, *this is stupid ghosts don't exist.*

So we went on the tour and were told to stay close to our teacher. It was a very cold and dark night and while we were walking my friend suddenly tripped. We fell behind and lost the others so we just carried on walking.

Suddenly we got to a dead end and we heard footsteps behind us. We turned around but we couldn't see anyone. We thought that it was our imaginations, but when we heard the footsteps again there was a figure standing there, just staring at us, dressed all in white. We tried to scream but we couldn't. As we tried the figure began to walk towards us. My friend looked at me all panicky and worried then she started to scream again. I wondered what I could do.

The figure was getting closer and closer. I could see its face, it was as white as a sheet and the eyes looked white. I looked round at my friend, she was still standing there but not moving. The ghost then came and touched me on the shoulder. I screamed and suddenly it disappeared.

Our class said that this was the most boring ghost trip ever because there weren't any ghosts. But we knew differently, we never forgot that night.

Kathryn Steinbrecher (12)
The Atherley School & Grove Place Preparatory School, Southampton

The Graveyard Secret

'David, I thought you said this was a good idea. Here we are in the middle of a graveyard, how could you ever have persuaded me to look for that gravestone at midnight … on Hallowe'en?'

He replied, 'Oh come on, it won't take long. Grow up, where's your sense of adventure? We're safe with Tess, she will bark if anything happens.'

'Can we go now David? I'm tired, cold, wet and hungry.'

'Wait … why is Tess barking? Maybe she has found something.'

They followed the dog until they found something quite shocking. They couldn't believe their eyes … an empty grave that hadn't been purposely dug up. This grave had been pushed up, the mounds of earth chucked everywhere. At that precise moment an owl hooted in the distance. An eerie shiver went down David's spine.

'Rachel, stop teasing me! Don't giggle, it's not funny.'

'I'm not giggling, more like screaming, don't you mean?'

'No, I definitely heard a giggle.'

'Right David, that's it I'm too scared. I'm going without you whether you like it or not.'

As Rachel started to walk off she heard a young child laughing. She turned around and witnessed David heading for the open grave, walking as if he were being led. Rachel heard Tess barking but knew she could do absolutely nothing at all. There was a deadly scream, one giggle and silence.

Neither Rachel or David were ever seen or heard of again, and Tess the dog was found blindly wandering the streets.

Alex Mostyn (13)
The Atherley School & Grove Place Preparatory School, Southampton

The Devil Doll

It watches me, it watches you, it watches everyone. You can't escape it, all you can do is hide, and even then it comes. You can only wait until she finds you ...

See, I got this great new china doll for Christmas, but after tonight, I'll wish I never did.

'Night Mum!' I shouted down the stairs.

'Night Thea!' she replied.

I carefully placed my doll on the rocking chair. She had shiny golden locks, with hypnotising bright blue eyes. She wore a pale blue frock with lace trimmings and little blue shoes.

I clambered into my bed on the other side of my room and buried myself in the covers.

I soon woke up to a rocking sound. It stopped. I was frightened, I hid under the covers. I slowly looked out again, the doll wasn't there! I gasped as I turned around and she was at the end of my bed. I stared into her deep blue eyes, she was motionless. 'I'm probably just seeing things,' I whispered to myself, but it was useless; I was trying to make myself believe something that I didn't think was the real truth. She seemed to stare at me, it was eerie.

I felt sick and woozy and my stomach was churning. Just as I started to close my eyes, the rocking sound started again and giggling, she disappeared. 'Where are you?' I shouted.

'Here!' she shouted as I felt something stroking my head.

I screamed, but no one heard.

Théa Carter (12)
The Atherley School & Grove Place Preparatory School, Southampton

Dreams To Nightmares

They left me in the house I'd always dreamed of ... But was it? I laid there struggling for breath as a pillow was forced over my face; it seemed like a lifetime. I finally broke free and ran into my parents' room, forgetting they weren't there!

The next day was as cold and dark as the house. The sun never rose, there was no flower in sight, nothing; just me. I went to the village to try and meet some people but it was like the town that time forgot; cobwebs everywhere, doors creaked. I just ran, the sooner I got home the better.

That night I was too scared to sleep in my room, so once again I slept in my parents'.

The following day I decided I couldn't go on living in fear so I rang my parents, but the wire was cut and I was certain I had not cut it. I couldn't find my mobile; someone must have taken it! Perhaps I didn't imagine that ghost smothering me with the pillow, maybe this was all actually real.

That night my parents arrived home early, but the strange thing was they ignored me when they got through the door. I followed them upstairs shouting at them, saying, 'Stop ignoring me, it's not funny. Come on, Mum, it's me. Seriously, stop it. Come on, it's not funny.'

They entered my room and there I was, laid on my bed, cold as ice. I was dead!

Sophie Hatchard (13)
The Atherley School & Grove Place Preparatory School, Southampton

Hospital

11th August 1989
Day Two

The hospital lights flicker then turn off. It is an eerie place when there is no light, to see the ugly laminate floor and the whitewashed windows of a typical hospital. I think I am the only one awake. It's so dark without those lights. I'm trying to go to sleep, because the nurses are telling me to. I can't though. I'm really vulnerable right now, so I'm on edge. I stopped a thief and he beat me up, then the police and an ambulance came. That was last night; now I'm here in London's General Hospital, while the thief is in custody. I'm trying to go to sleep now. Talk later.

That night, the hospital witnessed the horrible murder of John North, whose last entry is above. Unfortunately, the murderer committed suicide after this ghastly event. People say that their ghosts haunt the hospital. Mental patients here have claimed to have seen them, but it's still a mystery.

So enjoy your stay!

Emily Smith (13)
The Atherley School & Grove Place Preparatory School, Southampton

The Possessed Rag Doll

I was nine when it happened. My mum and I went to a second hand shop; it was there that I saw it. It was a beautiful gothic rag doll and I decided I must have it. We bought it and went home. I put it in my room by my bed. That night was when it all happened.

I woke up in the morning and rubbed my eyes. Along the wall in red writing was: *'I will kill you, Lucy, I will kill you!'* I screamed and my mum and dad came upstairs. We called the police but they could do nothing about it. I moved to my mum and dad's bedroom with my doll, but the same thing happened. I couldn't sleep at night.

Then one night, I was lying in my bed when I heard a cold laugh. Looking around I saw nobody apart from my doll. My mum and dad were snoring. I looked at the doll again; its eyes seemed to be glowing and there was a smirk on its face. I was petrified! It had a bracelet in its hand. I took it and put it on my wrist, I couldn't stop myself. I was thrown backwards and fainted. An overwhelming power hit me and I screamed frightfully.

I woke up in hospital. They had taken the bracelet off but no one could touch it without fainting. The doctors were mystified. I can never look at any rag doll again!

Meghan Brook (12)
The Atherley School & Grove Place Preparatory School, Southampton

A Point Of No Return?

It was a long dark day, there was a thick mist hanging over the sea. At that moment a ship, grey-silver, rolled in and stopped at the end of the cliff. Three people got on board: Mick, Raven and Dan. Raven was a tomboy. Once on board they entered a room full of furniture covered in dust sheets. At the back of the room there was a strange-shaped box. Raven went to look at it, when she vanished.

Mick and Dan were looking all over the ship when it started moving, then behind them they heard a low, loud breathing. They turned round to see Raven, with fangs. She had been turned into a vampire. Raven was holding a pendant. Mick and Dan turned to run but felt as if they were stuck. They managed to run into another room where there was a dressing table and a piece of paper with a riddle on it: 'The one that holds the pendant will be cursed and will never return to her normal form!'

Mick and Dan locked the door in hope that the vampire, or Raven, wasn't in there, but just seconds after they had locked the door it was there, the vampire. It ran at them both but it missed them, but it wasn't going to give up that easily. It grabbed Dan's hand and bit him. That was it, Mick was outnumbered now.

Francesca Solloway (13)
The Atherley School & Grove Place Preparatory School, Southampton

Her

When Giles' wife died, he cut himself off from the world. He boarded up his front door, all the windows, and lived by himself.

She was a pretty little soul and everyone cared about her a lot. The villagers felt so sorry for Giles and wanted to do anything they could to help him with is grief, but he wouldn't take their sympathy.

It was about three months after the death of his wife and for three months he'd been away from the world. There was no change in the way Giles acted and the grief hadn't ended.

A bang at the door alerted him one night. The door was still boarded up and no one had bothered him for about two months. He looked through the gap in one of the boards, but there was no one there. He pondered at the bottom of the staircase, then went back upstairs to bed. He slumped into bed and shut his eyes.

A tap on the window woke sleepy Giles, he ignored it though. Then he heard it again. His window flew open with his curtains flapping wildly. He grabbed his covers and wrapped them around him. The shutters banged and rattled as the wind blew them in all directions. Giles got out of bed and walked downstairs slowly; he heard the wind howling all through his house. As he reached the boarded door, the banging started. He looked through the tiny gap in the board and there she was ...

Livvi Ricketts (12)
The Atherley School & Grove Place Preparatory School, Southampton

I'm Scared

Julia was now alone as her parents had abandoned her for the weekend. It was now dark and Julia needed a light to see where she was, so she wandered up to the light switch, when the television flickered on and then off. She found a torch, but to Julia's luck, she had chosen the dud torch. Julia found a candle in the kitchen, so she lit it with the remaining matches and wandered over to one window sill where the curtains were swaying, even though there was no a breeze. She undid them ... nothing.

Julia had fallen asleep when she suddenly woke up with a jump. She got up and heard a heavy, long breath behind her. She looked around but nobody was there. She suddenly shivered and once again wandered around, nerves trembling. She heard a door banging. There was no one there though. Julia saw a giant shadow behind her head and was shaking with anxiety. Then a *swoosh* of wind came into the dull living area. Julia was gazing out of the window when she saw a white, floating object, which looked eerie. She got up and walked over to see what it was. She looked at the tree; there was nothing. Julia ran inside as she heard the phone, but when she picked it up there was no one on the line. She looked around and saw her mum and dad arriving ...

Anoushka Predko (13)
The Atherley School & Grove Place Preparatory School, Southampton

The Haunted Ghost Story

The house from a distance was black with cracked windows, the kind that looked like a bomb had gone off inside it and the remains and shingle were left.

Inside the house, I could feel something chilling blow down my neck all the way down my back. It was like the air inside had been frozen and hadn't moved for ages. There was a kind of mist afloat in the house, a cold, shimmering mist. Nothing breathed, just existed.

Every now and then I could have sworn I'd heard someone scream, as if in pain, maybe murder. And the effect afterwards was an eerie atmosphere in which I laid unsteadily.

I wandered around the house, gently disturbing the rotting wrecks of doors as they screeched in my face. Maybe this was a part of the screaming noise I'd heard, but who could be pushing the rotten planks? As I crept into different rooms there were chills oozing out of every tiny crack in the cobweb-covered floorboards.

Someone had not long left this place, the air in the room was not still and there was a disturbing silence which plagued my mind ...

Sophia Lingham (14)
The Atherley School & Grove Place Preparatory School, Southampton

The Faked Nightmare

A young couple decided to go on a holiday in Sweden in the winter holidays. They stayed in an empty hotel near a wood.

The first night, they couldn't sleep as they were being disturbed by the sound of unsteady walking and the jangling of keys outside their door along the corridor.

The next morning, they asked the hotel manager about the bizarre sounds and he told them the tale of the ghost of a madman who lived in a log cabin in the centre of the wood, who had died, frozen with his leg caught in a bear trap. The ancient manager hobbled away with his keys hanging out his pocket.

The next night they heard the noises again, but eventually slept. They were awoken at an early hour by an ear-splitting screech and then silence, quickly followed by cries for help which faded to nothing. They spied a strange patch on the ceiling developing fast, and soon it was dripping with blood. They were both shaking now and they heard the sound of footsteps getting louder and louder, until they stopped. The doorknob was twisting and the door was forced open.

'I'm very sorry about the noise. My daughter was having a nightmare,' the manager apologised.

By morning, the hotel was leaking pungent red blood. It has been said that the trees turned red and no one has set foot near the forest ever since.

Jemima Oosthuizen (14)
The Atherley School & Grove Place Preparatory School, Southampton

Whispering Trees

Steam and smoke mingled in the dappled twilight, swirling through the pine trees which gave the campsite where Jess and her family were staying its name. A silvery wisp in the corner of her vision separated itself from the rising mist and floated away, just above the dewy grass. Was she imagining it, or did this insignificant corkscrew of steam give a low, malicious hiss as it vanished into the gathering night? It certainly spiralled eerily as if it were slightly outside the realm of natural forces.

As she went to sleep that night, a pervasive hiss of steam penetrated the still air, above the creaking whisper of the wind as it rustled the tall trees surrounding the campsite.

Jess shivered as she tried to sleep that night, to a faint hissing, which could have been the sound of whispering wind blowing through the trees or not. There had been the steam, acting not quite usually, and everywhere, a faint whistling, bitter hiss, a hiss of malice.

There was a spine-chilling hiss, which drifted through the canvas of the tent. Jess gasped. A single drop of blood appeared in mid-air by her sleeping bag. Jess bent shakily over the drop as it descended slowly, coming to rest on the edge of her sleeping bag.

She ran from her tent and fumbled with the zip of her parents' tent. Her parents were dead; white as ghosts. And there was a single bloodstain on the floor.

Stephanie Williams (13)
The Atherley School & Grove Place Preparatory School, Southampton

That Night

I couldn't sleep that night. The wind was howling and the rain shattering against my window like a thousand bullets across the night sky. Suddenly, a sense of tiredness overcame my body, reaching through me like smoke, swirling around, filling space. I forgot who I was and became a mist, absorbing the scene of my child's bedroom, dark and empty apart from the life that lay heaped on the bed. A breeze ran through the house, lifting papers which then fluttered to the floor. I felt something approach, something strange. Not animal, not human, or anything from this world, and it was dangerous. I felt the blood drain out of my body as the spirit came towards the bedroom door. Drifting silently, shrouding everything it passed. I saw it floating menacingly towards the bed. My heart raced. I couldn't help, I wasn't there! Struggling, screaming for help, for someone to realise.

'Sarah! *Sarah!'*

I woke screaming in the night, cold sweat dripping off my pale face. All I could think about was *Sarah*. Mind racing, chest beating up and down, falling out of bed, the floor like quicksand, wishing, praying that it was just a dream. A play up of my thoughts. I reached the bedroom door, it was stuck. Breathing heavily, I shook the door violently, still screaming. I went mad at the thought of my dream coming true. The door broke and the minute after I looked into the room, I could no longer remember.

Isra Hawa (14)

The Atherley School & Grove Place Preparatory School, Southampton

Ghost Story

Turning sharp left, we entered 'Forbidden Lane'. Sure enough, 'Eerie Manor', lay straight in front, at the end of the undulating, rutted road. Shivering chills darted down my back as I saw it. The manor was an evil black.

There were a couple of houses on either side. Most of them deserted, except for one: number fourteen. An elderly woman came out of the house, making a cross with her hand, watching us to see which house we were to go in. She saw us drive into the manor. Before I turned round, she was gone.

Lightning, then thunder startled us whilst the car doors opened. Clutching my bags, I made it slowly towards the towering doors. Boris raced off, leaving me. I stepped on the aged door mat; creaking, both doors opened. Stepping in, not knowing what was going to happen. A man stood I front of me, pointing to my room.

The room was enormous. Strangely it was very beautiful compared to the rest of the house. Leaving my room to explore, I came across a room full of dead animals and models of people's heads. Unexpectedly, screams and shouts; noises came from all corners. Running towards the door, suddenly the lights went out. Darkness was all around me. Tumbling around the room, objects poked me. I screamed when colourless, dead faces appeared. One face started to chase me. Trying to run away was no use. Peeping over my shoulder, I recognized the face: the woman from house number fourteen.

Hilary Pegg (13)
The Atherley School & Grove Place Preparatory School, Southampton

The Disappeared

Callum and Cassy were asked by Mrs McKay, the head teacher, to write an article on the strange events in the school.

'I could describe how the store room locked itself and the light bulb went out. Then I could hear scratching, like the scratching of long fingernails on a blackboard,' said Cassy dramatically.

'And I could investigate the scratches on the wall,' said Callum.

While Callum was walking down Amber Street, he thought of the unearthly marks on the walls, when there was a spine-chilling chill in the wind. Along with the chill, a howl like a dog sounded. Feeling uncomfortable, but oblivious to what was following him, Callum thought, *why did I go this way?* The creature which was following him was the servant of a murderer looking for more followers.

Callum didn't know if he was dreaming, but he could have sworn that he saw hollow, red, burning eyes. Quickening his pace, Callum ran, and behind him he heard *s-l-a-p, s-l-a-p* of crusty, wet feet. He looked round, only to see tiger-sharp teeth, cracked, scabby skin and the same burning eyes. A merciful scream escaped from his mouth as a pair of long, infected nails swiped his face then its hands grabbed his mouth and dragged him into its lair.

Louise Brown (13)
The Atherley School & Grove Place Preparatory School, Southampton

Ghost Stories

'I'm coming to get you, you can't run, you can't move. I'm coming down your street now, I'm getting closer now, breathe your last breath now. I'm in your mind, I'm in your dream, you will not wake.'

Out of the window the dream flew, into the next house, taking lives, gaining energy. All it needed was enough children's lives to begin killing adults, then to be transported to an adult, and he could begin again. He came to the last house. 'Goodnight now, little child, and now I have enough and all in time.'

He flew to the next house as some light cracked up; this would kill the dream. He knew he was just too late, but if the girl didn't have a dream catcher, she wouldn't have shown the struggling thing to her parents.

Lydia Thomas (14)
The Atherley School & Grove Place Preparatory School, Southampton

Was It Or Was It Not?

'What's that noise? It sounds like there's a bell ringing,' said Tracy.

'Oh my goodness, you're right, and the sound is getting closer. Listen carefully!' Katie exclaimed.

'Are you crazy? Let's get out of here more like, we don't want to wait around to find out what's coming, I'm terrified enough. Please, can we just go back to your house, Tracy?' Stacy asked.

'You're such a scaredy-cat, Stacy. This old house can't really be haunted, that's just a story folk around here started to tell after the old lady died,' Tracy tried to calm down her friend.

'I don't care if it is just a story, it feels like someone or something is watching us, and that noise is getting louder and I want to get out of here.' Stacy was almost shouting at her friends in her eagerness to leave the old derelict house that she and her friends had come across in the woods they had gone walking in.

'Actually, for once I think you might be right, Stacy. I've got shivers up my spine and there's a very cold feeling creeping around me. Tracy, we'd better get going,' Katie suggested, with more than a little tremble in her voice.

'Oh, all right then, but honestly, I can't believe that you two really believe all that nonsense about ghosts and haunted houses and things. It doesn't bother me at all,' Tracy replied.

'If this house isn't haunted, then what's that?' Katie screamed and pointed to the door ...

Miffy Gradwell (12)
The Ladies' College, Guernsey

I Long To Sleep

All was silent. Nobody was awake. No one stirred, except for me. But does that really count? I am not sure. But then I am not sure of anything anymore. Not since - since it happened. But I won't speak of that.

I went on a tour of the house. This is what I fill my time with now. I make commentary on it. 'And now for the master bedroom. Note beautiful oak furniture and lavish bedclothes with matching curtains.' Sometimes I make a game of it; how many chairs I can touch in a minute. How many people can I see?

I used to wish I could slip downstairs, unnoticed, to watch TV without my parents knowing, or to steal a piece of cake, or to take the cat upstairs to my room where he wasn't allowed. Now I long to be caught hiding behind the sofa, watching TV when I should be in bed. I long to hear my mother say, 'Oh Harold, go to your room, you naughty boy'. As I creep around the corridors, I long for someone to spot me and put me back to bed. I long to sleep.

Light is starting to peep through the curtains. I look at the clock. Almost seven. I hear a voice, my sister's voice, 'Oh, Harry, I miss you. Come back, Harry. Why did you have to die?'

Kirsten Anderson (12)
The Ladies' College, Guernsey

A Son Comes Home

It started when the Mawsons rented the house. It was an old family home, but the owner had moved to America.

The first time it happened was very soon after they moved in. On their first day, in fact. Lucy Mawson was in her new bedroom. She looked up and saw a man. He was dressed in unusual clothes: a black kaftan, indigo leggings and electric-blue boots. He was tall and skinny and had long, greasy, dark brown hair. He stood staring at her for ten, maybe twenty seconds, and ran out of the room. She heard footsteps as he ran downstairs and the bang of a door.

'Barney!' she shouted to her husband, Barnabas, running downstairs. 'Did you see that man?'

'Yeah, the guy in the black top and funny boots? I saw him, Luce. What's he doing in our new home?'

'I dunno, Barn, but he gave me the creeps. Something about him made me shake.' Lucy was shaken alright, you could hear it in the way she spoke.

The owner's mother was round the next day to check how they were settling in. Lucy had told her about the strange man over the phone and she'd brought something to show them.

'The man you described sounded a lot like my son and I've brought a photo of him for you to see,' she explained.

'Yup, that's definitely the guy. I thought he was living in Chicago?'

The woman looked white. 'He was, until the car crash.'

Shona Walne (10)
Widewell Primary School, Plymouth

Is She My Friend?

One time I woke up and looked out of the window. I saw a ghostly figure, it looked like someone I knew, but I wasn't quite sure so I went outside to see who it was and no, it couldn't be … it was my friend and she was a ghost.

I went up to her and she got up. I said, 'Why are you … ?'

'Well, I'm dead,' she replied. 'I got run over and I can't tell you who did it, but I'll get my revenge on her.'

I started to shiver, then suddenly she came and went right through me, so I ran after her but she was already in the house. Before I could stop her, she had already killed her, my dear old sister. There she lay, dead on the floor. I burst into tears and my no-longer friend, who killed her, disappeared away to her grave.

Sydnie Anstey (10)
Widewell Primary School, Plymouth

The Cursed Doll

Once upon a time there was a doll, sat on a shelf in a toy shop. Unfortunately, a curse had been put on the pretty doll with huge black eyes by an evil shop owner.

One day, a little girl called Sarah bought the doll with her birthday money and took her home. That night, Sarah took her beautiful doll in the lacy black dress up to her bedroom and sat her beside her bed so she would be close by while she slept.

Next morning when Sarah woke, the doll had gone. She searched everywhere but couldn't find her. She cried as she told her mum and dad. They were puzzled because Sarah had been unwell for two days and had not been out of her bedroom. Sarah realised she'd been dreaming and forgot about the doll.

Years later, Sarah returned to her parents' home with her own daughter, Sam. Sam decided to explore the house and found her mother's old bedroom. Beside the bed was a beautiful doll with huge black eyes and a black lacy dress. Sam ran downstairs to tell her mother what she'd found. Sarah was amazed when Sam described the doll she had once played with in her dreams. The doll was nowhere to be seen, just like before. The curse lives on!

Joshua Chandler (10)
Widewell Primary School, Plymouth

The Haunted Castle

Hello, my name is Emily. One day, me and my brother, Ben, were looking in the attic. We suddenly saw an old dusty map in a dusty box. On the map it had a picture of a castle called Widewell Castle. It looked scary. It also said there was treasure to be found in the castle. My brother and I decided to find the treasure, so we set off.

It was a long journey. We walked through a dark wood, which was spooky. Finally, we got to the castle through a big, heavy wooden door. The door slammed behind us and it made my brother and I jump! We started to walk around the castle ...

Suddenly, we heard a door slam! It was a bright light; it was a ghost! My brother and I screamed and ran away. I held Ben's hand and we walked up some steep steps. Suddenly, we heard a noise and a ghost jumped around from a corner. The ghost had chains hanging from his arms. My brother started to cry, so we ran off as fast as we could. When we were down the steep steps, we checked the map and realised we were really close to the treasure. My brother and I had to reach the highest point of the castle. Then we saw a sparkle coming through a gap under the door. It was the *treasure!*

Emily Piper (11)
Widewell Primary School, Plymouth

Young Writers Information

We hope you have enjoyed reading this book - and that you will continue to enjoy it in the coming years.

If you like reading and writing poetry and short stories drop us a line, or give us a call, and we'll send you a free information pack.

Alternatively, if you would like to order further copies of this book or any of our other titles, then please give us a call or log onto our website at **www.youngwriters.co.uk**

Young Writers, Remus House, Coltsfoot Drive, Woodston,
Peterborough PE2 9JX
Tel (01733) 890066

Email youngwriters@forwardpress.co.uk